ICE
REGULATORS MC

Chelsea Camaron
& Jessie Lane

She's an investment banker.

He's an outlaw biker.

A little bit of heaven is about to meet a whole lot of hell.

Morgan Powell was raised to be perfect, to set the example for her sisters to follow. Her life is dedicated to making something of her career so she wouldn't know what to do with a man even if you gave her an instruction manual.

Brett 'Ice' Grady spends his days trying to keep up with his teenage daughter and his nights consumed in Regulators' MC business. He has no time for anything more than a casual hookup.

Two worlds collide when the dangers of his life crash into the calm of hers.

Can she go beyond her own boundaries and chip her way through to the man to be known as cold as ice?

Ice

Regulators MC Series #1
By Chelsea Camaron & Jessie Lane
Copyright © 2014 by Chelsea Camaron & Jessie Lane
Published by Whiskey Girls Publishing

Edited by C&D Editing & Asli Fratarcangeli
Cover Design by Mina Carter
Cover Images by: © Furious Fotog | Golden Czermak
Cover Model: Shawn Dawson

Coming in 2015!

<u>Hammer</u> – Regulators MC Series #2 – March 2015

<u>Coal</u> – Regulators MC Series #3 – June 2015

For more information on Chelsea and her books check out her website:

http://www.authorchelseacamaron.com

Or you can send Chelsea Camaron an email at:

chelseacamaron@gmail.com

For more information on Jessie and her books check out her website: http://jessielanebooks.com/

Or you can send Jessie Lane an email at:

jessie_lane@jessielanebooks1.com

Other Titles From Whiskey Girls Publishing

By Chelsea Camaron

One Ride
Forever Ride
Merciless Ride

Maverick

Crash and Burn
Restore My Heart
Salvaged
Full Throttle
Beyond Repair
Stalled

Kale (co-written with Theresa Marguerite Hewitt)

By Jessie Lane

Secret Maneuvers
Stripping Her Defenses

Big Bad Bite
Walk On The Striped Side

The Burning Star
The Frozen Star

ICE

Book 1, Regulators MC Series

Chelsea Camaron
& Jessie Lane

Whiskey Girls
Publishing

Chapter
1

Ice

"Suck harder. Right there… Fuck yeah, that's it."

The half-naked platinum blonde kneeling in front of me sucks dick like a damn champ.

"Shit! Dammit, Dad!" my teenage daughter, Brooke, suddenly shrieks from across the living room while covering her eyes with her hands. Her voice immediately kills my hard on.

Pushing the bimbo off me, I stand to pull up my pants, wincing as I tuck my still sensitive cock away. I move forward to go find my daughter, who is not supposed to be home today. The blonde paws at me as I go to make my way past her. I would have preferred it if she would have run her mouth and taken off; instead, she is pouting at me because we didn't finish. I wish Brooke could have just given me five more minutes to get off. Then I could have gotten rid of the broad on her knees. Tossing this barfly out the door would be a hell of a lot easier then.

"Get out. I'm done with ya," I dismiss her, tired of the sulking look on her face. Damn woman, take a hint already.

With a huff, she rights her clothes, collects her things, and scurries out.

After making my way down the hall, of my not so modest home, I bark a sardonic laugh when I turn the knob to my daughter's room and find it locked.

"Open this door, young lady," I order, in what comes out as a bellow. We have danced this dance on more than one occasion.

"Sorry, I'm busy searching for the eye bleach. I can't unlock the door right now, check back later."

"Don't make me kick it in. You want to go without a door again? Don't traumatize us both. I don't want to pass by and see you in your skivvies any more than you want me to... or worse, for Hammer to catch you."

I am hoping like hell she listens. Last time, I took the damn door right off the frame. Later on, I wished I hadn't, though. It ended up punishing me as much as her when I had to listen to that boy band garbage she calls music.

Within seconds, I hear her feet stomping over. There is a click, a turn of the knob, and then my one true love in this life glaring at me. The door may have won the first round, but this victory is mine. Having a teenager, I have learned to celebrate every win, no matter how small.

"Brooke, what the fuck have I told you about your mouth? Young ladies shouldn't cuss! It makes you sound like a damn delinquent." I chastise for her mouth when she first walked in. She was supposed to be at an afterschool study group. Teenagers, never following their damn schedules.

"Yeah, Dad, real good speech you're givin'. Father of the year material, you are."

"Don't you get smart with me," I say, knowing it is falling on deaf ears, not that I should be surprised. My mom did always liked to rub it in my face that Brooke gets her stubbornness from me.

"Anyways"—her tone is just as sharp as before—"now that you've kicked the dog out, what are we doin' for dinner?"

That is Brooke: my sixteen-year-old daughter, my life, my world, and my eternal pain in the ass. If her mom was still alive, maybe things would be different. Maybe. Only I don't have time to play should-a, could-a, would-a in my head, because I am too busy raising her on my own.

Erin, Brooke's mom, was Brooke's age when she got pregnant. We were young and dumb. Obviously, we didn't think of protecting ourselves or give a second thought to plans for the future. Condoms were preached to us, birth control, all that. Yet, when the time came, we went at each other like rabbits and never gave a second thought to all that shit people had lectured us about.

When the little stick showed a pink line, I puked and Erin cried. Her parents immediately kicked her out and never got past it. With no job, no education, and nowhere to go, she moved in with my mom and me.

My mom was determined we would both finish high school. Stepping up to help us in every way she could, she worked two jobs to cover daycare costs and then spent many nights up with baby Brooke so Erin and I could study or do homework. I was a senior and Erin a junior in high school. It wasn't easy, but we made it through. Having a family to support, I graduated and joined the Army right after Erin and I got married.

Leaving Erin and a barely one-year-old Brooke behind was hard; yet I was focused on having a career to support us, not only a paycheck. My mom was supportive of my young wife, helping out with Brooke as I was now gone more than I was home. Selection to Special Forces was hard, training even harder, but having my green beret was everything. I developed pride in myself, pride in my country, pride for my family, and pride in joining together with my brothers to give our all to something more than ourselves. Young? Naïve? Yes, I was. However, drive, dedication, and commitment to my team were what pushed me through the realities of my situation.

I had thought life was going well for my family. I was making something of myself in the Army, somebody my wife and child could be proud of. Erin was supportive during my deployments and missions. She was always quick to show me how much she loved me. My mom was enjoying the time she spent with both Erin and Brooke.

Then the red-cross message came in while I was on a mission in Kosovo. When on a mission, communication to and from home is limited, to say the least. There was no direct line to reach me. My mom followed protocol and used the red-cross to send the devastating news to my Command, who then allowed it to trickle down to me.

Erin was hit by a drunk driver. D-O-A, dead on arrival.

She was nineteen years old with an almost three-year-old little girl at home, and just like that, she was gone.

The woman who hit her was leaving a kid's birthday party with her own two children in tow. According to the police report, she admitted to having a few glasses of wine at the party. The toxicology report showed a blood alcohol level double the legal limit. Doesn't matter what any of the reports say; bottom line, she walked away with only minor injuries and her children. Meanwhile, my daughter will never get the chance to really know her mom.

It is the epitome of a fucked-up tragedy.

Brooke will never see, for herself, the way Erin used to smile down at her as she fell asleep. Tuck the blankets around her little body. Sing her a lullaby. Kiss her on the forehead goodnight.

She will never hear the melodic sounds of her mother's laughter. God, I loved Erin's laugh. It was loud and beautiful. Anyone who heard it either stopped and stared or laughed along with her.

Brooke had no mom to explain her body to her. That was a nightmare for me, of epic proportions. What man wants his teenaged daughter to ask him when she will start her period? I still shudder every time I remember that awkward conversation. Or, I should say, lack of conversation because I immediately called my mother and told her to handle that shit. I don't talk about periods with the women I fuck, so I sure as shit am not going to talk about it with my daughter.

She had no mom to do her hair for her first homecoming dance or go dress shopping with her. Instead, I sprang for her to go to a well-known hairstylist and asked my mom to help her pick out a dress. I have already decided, for prom this year, I will give her my cash, and she can shop with her friends. When she comes home, she will twirl around in her dress, much like she did when she was a little girl, and I will tell her she is beautiful.

Brooke will never be able to see for herself that she is her mother's daughter. No, my daughter misses all of this and so much more, all because of the poor choices of one individual.

My mom stepped up after Erin's death, practically raising Brooke until I got out of the Army. That was when my mom got the news of her cancer, and I had to step up. I had always been an active part of Brooke's life while I was home, but then it was time to tackle twenty-four-seven single parenthood.

Needless to say, Brooke and I are still adjusting, especially after Mom lost her battle with cancer, not quite six months ago. It has been hard, my lifestyle making it more challenging; however, there is nothing I wouldn't do for my baby girl.

Thinking about my mom and the influence she had on Brooke, I can't help smiling. She did her best to teach

Brooke, guiding her into young womanhood. She did not only instill in Brooke how to have confidence and be an independent girl, but also the basics around the house she was afraid I wouldn't teach as a man.

"You could cook, ya know? Grams taught you to bake cookies and shit," I remind my teen.

Brooke laughs her mother's laugh. "Shit- if I cook, that's what you're gonna get for dinner- Shit."

In my days in the Army, I had enough MREs— Meals Ready to Eat—and tasteless chow hall grub to last me a lifetime. There is no way I want to risk a dinner that tastes that bad again.

"Steakhouse or Mexican?" I ask, turning to make my way back down the hall.

"Mexican," she replies, running past me to grab her helmet, letting me know she wants to take the bike.

Spoiled rotten little shit. She knows I won't deny her.

Morgan

Looking at my phone screen, I smile at the text in front of me.

I'm off 2nite. Movie @ ur house or mine?

Texting back, I tell my best friend I will be at her house after work with takeout. Working in a bank, I have every weekend off. Casey's career path is far different than mine, though, and it is one that requires weekend time; as a result, this is the first Friday she has had off in a while.

My day drags on as I review current investment portfolios and market changes. I have the best job ever. I get paid to spend other people's money as an investment broker here in South Beach. My life is sun, sand, and dollar bills.

Before going to Casey's, I stop by my condo and change clothes. The down side to my job is the stuffy suits I have to wear: reasonable, past knee-length skirts, reasonable women's dress pants, and reasonable button up shirts. I might hate them; yet, in a sad way, the dress code fits my life—reasonable.

It is not long into girl's night before the difference in our lifestyle's show.

"Damn, we're not even halfway through the first movie, and you're ready for bed? What the hell? Grandparents stay up later than you," My best friend wakes me out of my doze.

"Sorry, some of us keep normal business hours."

"Yeah, your hours scream forty-two, not twenty-four, as does everything else in your life."

"I'm not that bad," I protest half-heartedly. However, that voice of doubt says "maybe I am." Maybe my stiff upbringing has rubbed off on me more than I care to admit.

My parents raised me to be an example. As the oldest of three, I had to be the light to guide my younger sisters, Madyson and Mallory. Everything with my parents was about fitting the mold, keeping up appearances. Their brainwashing worked to some degree. Going away to college did nothing for me in my attempt to escape my overbearing parents, either. No, they live in my head, every rule engraved into my brain matter. Too bad no one warned me there is no cure and no escape once they get those rules engrained into my very being.

Morgan Ann Powell: pathetic, stiff, borderline pseudo-old lady, and a college educated, suit wearing, have my shit together prude—that is me. I am, quite possibly, the only woman in her twenties who can count on one hand how many guys she has kissed. I am also a twenty-four-year-old virgin. I wouldn't know what to do with a penis if it was given to me gift wrapped in Christmas paper and topped with a bow. I am not cut out for parties, guys, or any wild times, either. My destiny is to be the old lady who lives alone, feeding all the stray cats in the neighborhood.

"I'm a loser." Sighing, I look over to my best friend. "Sorry for ruining your night off."

"Stop it! You aren't a loser, and nothing is ruined. I was dozing off, too."

"Yeah, but it's not often you get a Friday night off. Spending it on the couch with your socially inept friend isn't an ideal night."

Slapping my thigh, she laughs. "With everything I see at the club, a night in is heaven."

Aside from being my drop-dead gorgeous best friend, Casey also happens to be a headlining stripper at a local club, After Midnight. Her perky, full breasts, tiny waist, and hips give her the picture-perfect, hourglass figure. Her long, black hair is streaked in purple and teal, adding to the illusion of the wild woman she portrays on the stage. Her curves fall in all the right places, suiting her perfectly and making for optimal tips in her chosen profession. "Work with what you have been given," she always says. And boy, does she work. Inside, Casey is as calm and happy to stay at home as me.

That is basically all we have in common, though. I could never have the sort of confidence she has. My parents raised me to be reserved in appearances. Where Casey dares to flash her pin-up body in tight clothes, I hide my own curves behind much more conservative attire. I also keep my make-up minimal, only using enough to naturally accentuate my creamy skin and moss green eyes.

Casey often lets her long, gorgeous hair down in wild curls. I, generally, keep my straight shoulder length, russet brown hair in a bun or a ponytail. I cannot count how many times I have wished I had her confidence. However, every time I try to push myself to be more daring with my appearance, I hear one of my mother's many lectures in the back of my head. There are days I wonder if I need to have a priest do an exorcism to cleanse me of her unrealistic ideals.

My best friend and I also had two completely different childhoods. While I grew up with strict parents and an overly structured life, she grew up with an ailing grandmother. Her dad is unknown and her mom overdosed when she was six, leaving a young Casey with her grandmother. When Nana died, while we were teens, Casey ended up in foster care.

She was fortunate. None of the horror stories of abuse and neglect happened to her in the many homes she was bounced between. The problem she faced was that, at eighteen, she had been tossed out. Sink, swim, or when all else fails, strip.

Casey worked a few of the nasty clubs to begin with. After Midnight won't take just anyone off the street, and she had no dance experience whatsoever. It was hard to watch her struggle before she found her way there. She was at the lowest of the low to begin with, places where the girls aren't given choices and anything goes.

Things changed when she got the job at After Midnight. The club has rules for the girls and the patrons. She is well protected and paid, and she actually enjoys her job. Other than the occasional drunk grabby guy, Casey doesn't come home with bruises anymore.

I have offered for her to live with me, time and time again, through the years, even in college. My parents paid for not only my education, while I was earning my degree, but my apartment and expenses, as well. I begged Casey to come with me, and we would find a way to make it work for her. However, she is stubborn and independent to a fault and refuses any type of handout.

She wants to make it all on her own, and I applaud her determination. It took her a little longer than me. However, at the end of this semester, I will be there, proudly watching my very best friend receive her degree in sports medicine. She took the long, hard road less traveled and made it happen for herself.

She is a fierce beauty, a fierce woman, and she has fierce loyalty—everything I am not.

ICE

Chapter

2

Ice

Offices make me jittery. Unfortunately, they are a necessary evil for running a business. Paperwork—some nights I feel like I drown in the shit.

Kara used to help keep me straight on both of our strip clubs. She kept the administrative bullshit off my plate, kept the dancers out of my face, and did it all with such attitude it made my dick hard. I really miss having her around, and not only for the times she warmed my bed.

With one look at Sullivan, everything I had with her was over. Those two had unfinished business, history, and more emotion shared between them than I have seen in my lifetime.

She has her life with him now. Doesn't mean I don't think about what we could have had if her ex hadn't shown up bringing with him all their unfinished business. Would I have ever given her hearts and flowers? Fuck no. That is not me. I would have given her security and happiness and a warm body in bed with her at night, though. Fidelity. She also would have had the security of knowing she wasn't alone. With a woman like Kara at home, you sure as shit don't need or want a barfly.

Sometimes I could see a bleakness surrounding her like an emotional armor. It kept her from connecting with others, living her life. However, when I had her on the back of my bike, she shed that armor and embraced life.

I might not be able to give her the sort of emotions women usually want, but I would have given her a good life. A woman like her deserves to be happy. I would have been honored to be the man to give her that. Not that I am some unselfish hero or some shit. Hell no. Sometimes, a man gets tired of being lonely. Problem is, I hadn't come across a woman, until Kara, that I would have been willing to tie myself down to after my wife had died.

My casual affair with Kara lasted a few years after she had stopped working at After Midnight. The woman has a mind for business and could work a pole like no other. She came to me shy, defeated, and a shell of a human being. Watching her grow, transform, and come into her own was something books should be written about. She fought with everything inside her to pull out of the depths of the hell depression had sucked her into. I was damn proud of her. I have seen grown men in the military that couldn't handle the kind of demons she had and come out of it alive. Kara is now a curvy, knockout package, carrying a warrior's heart; the kind of woman men around the world over would live and die for.

Riley Sullivan, her ex-husband—now her soon-to-be husband again, the real light of her life, soul mate, whatever—is one lucky bastard to have her. Kara moved to Virginia to be with Sullivan a little over three months ago. If he ever takes it for granted or fucks it up, I will be there to remind him exactly how good he had it. I will know the minute Sullivan fucks up because I have kept tabs on her, discreetly, through weekly check-ins with my old Army buddy, Lucas Young, who works on the same black ops unit, the Ex Ops Team, as Sullivan.

The Ex Ops Team came down to Miami and did an undercover gig with information my boys and I had dug up on missing women in our area. They ended up leaving with their mission half-finished to regroup and bury two of their men; although, not before they were able to get the name of a man who might be connected to the missing women—Lazaro Sandoval. What Lucas and his team don't know is that the Regulators have picked up where they left off. We are on a mission of our own now.

The music changes, drawing my thoughts back to my office and the budget needing my attention. After Midnight is our female strip club, the place I prefer to spend my time. To corner the market on both sides of legally selling skin, we also have Alibi, an all-male strip establishment for the ladies to come toss their dollar bills around. The Regulators MC has to have some sort of legitimate business front—enter the two clubs for us. To keep the damn Internal Revenue Service off our asses, I make sure the books stay on point. We wouldn't want some of our not so legitimate business associates to look into us and find anything off point, either. Tonight, it is my night to update Alibi for the month.

The music changes once again, this time to Shane's opening song. The lyrics make me shake my head. Why in the world bitches would want to ride on a 'disco stick,' I don't know. What I do know is Shane makes more money off that routine than any of the other boys that strip here.

Hearing the ridiculous fucking song, I know it means I won't be stepping out of this office anytime soon if I can help it. Seeing another man's dick swinging around is fucked-up when you don't swing that way. Almost enough to traumatize me, and I saw some seriously screwed up shit when I was in the Army. Not to mention I had to see more hairy asses in the communal showers during my service than a ninety-year-old woman sees during the course of her marriage.

Then it hits me. Shane is headlining this week. If he is going on stage, then it is around eleven. Looking at my phone, I am met with a blank screen. No new notifications. Brooke is required to be home by her curfew, which is ten on school nights and eleven on weekends. I know it is far from freedom, but the later it gets, the more things she could get into that she shouldn't. With the late nights I keep, it is necessary for Brooke and me to have a system in place. She is supposed to call me from our home phone, that way I know she is tucked safely away inside our house.

Dialing my landline phone at home, I feel the tension rise in me with every ring that goes unanswered. The life of an outlaw biker is hard enough on its own; however, being a single dad to a teenage daughter is a never ending nightmare. Combine the two, and I am one trigger happy bastard.

We live in a gated community already, but I have a security system installed that could rival the White House. Even then, I keep a prospect on watch if I am going to be any later than midnight. My lifestyle isn't conducive to parenthood, and Brooke could be used for leverage against me. No, I don't raise her in a perfect scenario, though I do the best I can to give her a better future. It is what it is, and we make it work... well, usually.

Calling her cell phone, I am more on edge when she doesn't answer that, either. Met with her perky voice recording, adrenaline kicks in.

"You got me. Leave a message at the beep if you're hot," Brooke's teen voice radiates in my ears.

"Oh, I got you all right. You best believe I'm hot, too. Only it's the kind of hot that's going to get your ass grounded for a month. Call me, Brooke, before I come find you. If I have to come looking for you, little girl, we're going to have serious problems."

Rather than waste another minute, I use the app on my smart phone to track hers. She may think she knows everything, but she has no clue. Teenagers—*sigh*—they don't understand the real dangers that lurk, the bad things that can easily happen in the blink of an eye.

Recognizing the address on the screen, I see it is one of the upper class neighborhoods in our area. My heart pounds wildly in my chest. She obviously isn't studying at Janessa's, since she only lives two doors down from us, and this is showing her phone is not on our street.

Stepping out of my office, the noise of the club assaults my ears. The sounds of women screeching alerts me that Shane must be taking something off. Thank heavens for that warning; it lets me know to keep my eyes on the bar as I make my way out.

Catching a glance over at Hammer and Coal, I give a quick chin lift. My silent acknowledgement immediately has them jumping from their stools to follow me.

Without a word shared between us, we all climb on our bikes and take off. We share a bond of brotherhood. They trust me to lead them straight through the depths of any hell, even the parenthood of a daughter. In turn, I trust them to have my back, and, most importantly, to keep me from killing a teenage boy for merely looking at my baby girl.

At the entrance to the subdivision, I easily maneuver my bike around the bar meant to keep people out. When the overweight security guard steps outside of his stand, I flip him my middle finger. He can call the cops, no problem. The Miami-Dade police department won't touch me, especially not for picking up my disobedient daughter. Not to mention that I have connections so far above their pay grade it would make them piss their pants.

Riding farther into the upscale development, the noise of the party drowns out even my motorcycle pipes. I am surprised the stuffy suits that live in places like this haven't called the cops themselves.

Easily following the sounds, I find the three story deluxe home with cars packing the driveway. Parking my bike on the edge of the road, I hop off with Hammer and Coal following suit. They don't bother asking questions, because my reason for coming here is obvious as we make our way into a house full of drunken teens.

Walking inside like I own the place, I see kids in every corner, making out. The sight makes my blood boil.

If I find some little dipshit with his hands all over my baby girl, it is going to take both Hammer and Coal to keep me from beating the shit out of him. I don't care if they are teenagers; no little prick is good enough to touch Brooke.

I glance into the formal dining room to my left, and someone has one very expensive table that seats eight, making a perfect set up for beer pong. Jesus, this is the nightmare of every parent. If I see one kid doing any drugs, my head is going to explode.

"Brooke," I call out. "Brooklyn Rayne Grady, get your ass out here… Right. The. Fuck. Now!" I roar without a second thought.

All the teens stop and stare at me and my brothers filling up this ostentatious entryway. When nobody moves, Coal steps up to be right behind me on the left.

"Brooke, find her now," Coal clips out, giving his cold glare to every teen in the room.

At the top of the stairway, I watch my daughter meet Coal's gaze without one ounce of trepidation. Baby girl is showing balls of steel for her friends. Her short as sin shorts make my blood pressure shoot up even higher. The camisole tank top that I bought to go with pajamas is far from hiding her buds from all these teen pricks.

"Dad—" she starts as I interrupt.

"Don't say another fucking word. Get your ass on my bike."

"Death of you," Hammer chuckles behind me as he turns around to get ready to leave.

Yes, my daughter will be the death of me. I watch as she grabs her friend by the wrist and half drags her down the stairs, mumbling at her the whole way down. When the two girls reach me, I don't move.

"Come on, Dad," Brooke lets out a huff. "Let's go. This is embarrassing enough already."

"Everybody here, you have twenty minutes to get this house cleaned the fuck up. Since you dumb shits have been drinking, a bus will be here to pick each one of you up and take you home. My man Coal here is gonna stay behind and make sure you do as I say."

"Daaaad," Brooke whines, "leave everyone alone."

"Brooke, I suggest you shut your mouth and get your ass over to my bike. If your friend needs a ride, Hammer will take her. Outside. Now. You're in enough trouble, don't add more."

Defeated, the two girls stomp off while Hammer shakes his head at me while I turn to follow them all out. I haven't even made it to the door when I hear some pre-pubescent shithead slur out a question.

"Do you think they are, like, real biker dudes? Maybe we can ask them to pop a wheelie or something. WAIT!" His voice cracks as he gets excited. "Maybe they're from that show on TV! We should ask for their autographs!'

God save me from teenagers. No doubt, Hammer is cussing me out in his head for sticking one on his bitch seat.

Morgan

Bam. Bam. Bam.

Ding. Dong.

Ding. Dong.

Bam. Bam. Bam.

The rapid percussions of someone at my door startles me awake. Grabbing my pepper spray from my nightstand, I sit up and get out of bed. No one visits me unexpectedly. Ever. Not even Casey. My neighbors must have misplaced guests, or maybe this is some crazy prank.

Looking out my peephole, I see a man in a black shirt, a black leather vest with a patch that says "ICE", and jeans. His brown hair is short on the sides yet a little longer on the top. Before I can inspect him through the tiny hole longer, he is pounding on my door again, making me jump.

Twisting the safety piece, I ready my pepper spray as I twist the lock on my door. I don't even get my hand on the knob to turn it before I am being pushed back by my door opening.

Raising my arm, I ready to spray when my wrist is suddenly wrapped in a firm grip and my hand quickly and efficiently emptied of its contents. So much for my self-defense savviness.

"This one belong to you?" the rugged looking stranger gruffly asks me as he points his thumb over his shoulder, obviously pissed. There is another man with him. His vest has a patch that says "HAMMER" and a teen girl shifting nervously beside him.

Taken aback by his terse attitude, I stand there for a moment, frozen and unsure of what to do. His eyes are so dark and lethal looking I can't tell if they are black or brown. The harsh lines of his face accentuate his high cheekbones that are flushed in anger, and his strong jaw is clenched tight. I can't decide if he is drop dead sexy, in a scary sort of way, or just plain scary. My chest rapidly rises and falls as I struggle to catch up with everything happening. Following his pointed finger, my eyes land on my sister.

Madyson, my drop dead gorgeous, just turned eighteen, high school senior, little sister is standing in my doorway. Her eyes plead with me to take her.

What the heck did she get herself tangled up in now? Why did she bring this to my doorstep? Our parents expect bad things from her; therefore, this would be nothing unusual. However, I don't expect her to bring her problems to me.

"Ummm," I begin, but I am cut off.

"Ummm, nothin'. She gave us this address to drop her off at. Since you obviously aren't old enough to be her mother, I'm goin' to assume she's your sister. There is a similarity in your features. Clue in, sweets; girls at this age shouldn't be out this late and certainly not dressed like a hooker. Know where your girl is. Take responsibility, for fuck's sake. Bad things can happen," He releases my wrist harshly and turns to walk away.

Something changes inside me. I should stay quiet and let him leave, but I can't. "Take responsibility? You don't know me, mister, don't judge me."

Looking over his shoulder, his cold stare meets mine. "I didn't fuckin' stutter. Take responsibility. She's yours. She's carefree and breathing. Keep her home, keep her dressed, and that'll keep her carefree and breathing."

My sister steps into my condo as the stranger makes his way out without ever looking back.

"Seriously? Seriously! I can't believe you, Madyson! Why did you bring your problems to my doorstep?" I yell hysterically, not worrying about my neighbors or what the stranger may hear.

"Mom and Dad," she croaks out. "I'm always the disappointment, and I didn't want to deal with it tonight. Give me a break, please," She is begging me. I can't stand when she does this—uses me as her hiding spot when she has done something wrong and doesn't want to face our parents who expect too much, yet always make us feel as if we never measure up.

I don't know what to say or do. I am half asleep and not prepared for any of this tonight.

Sighing in defeat, I tell her, "Go to bed. Call Mom and tell her you're over here. Then go home tomorrow." Not waiting for her reply, I lock up quickly and retreat to my room.

ICE

Chapter

3

Ice

"Screech, run Madyson Leigh Powell through all channels. She just turned eighteen. Hopefully there won't be anything, but I want her entire life on my desk tonight," I order into my phone.

Screech is our computer guru, hacker, IT guy, or whatever-the-hell title he chooses to go by. I don't give a shit what he calls himself as long as he keeps doing what I need him to do. The man is a genius on web searches, hiding information that needs to stay buried, deleting information that needs to not exist, and creating false paper trails when the time calls for it. He is tall, lanky, and socially awkward. His crazy curly brown hair, glasses, and nut hugging skinny jeans he chooses to wear don't make him the typical Regulator. He is loyal and a borderline genius. I trust him with my life, in his own way. With a few taps on his keyboard, he could ruin someone's life as they know it.

I try to give Brooke some space about her friends. I try to be the 'normal' dad as much as I can, knowing what I know about people and doing what I do for a living. Seeing the lowest of the low, the scumbags that walk day in and day out, side by side with regular everyday citizens, warps one's perception of the world and everyone in it. For me, it is a battle not to run checks on every person Brooke comes into contact with. I give her room. I don't automatically search them, but the second they give me a reason to, I am all over it.

Girls. They seem to change their friends like they do their damn panties. Madyson is Brooke's "bestie," as she says. I don't give a fuck what she is called. I want to know what her story is. Hell, I want to know her whole family's story, every last one of them.

Why is she living with her sister? Why were the girls at the party last night? Does she get good grades? Thousands of questions race through my mind concerning this girl and her influence on my daughter.

Walking into After Midnight, I am glad for the early afternoon quiet. Brooke is not happy about being grounded, to say the least. In turn, this means a lot of stomping, screaming, and all out noise around my house to show her displeasure.

"Thought I'd find you here," a female voice purrs from behind me.

Turning around, I am faced with Tonya, Tammy, Tanya, something close to that. She is a barfly I have hooked up with a few times. She hasn't been around lately, though.

"Well, you got me. Now, what're you gonna do with me?" I ask with a wink.

She makes her way over to me and then trails her fingers seductively down my cut and lower. "I'm down for anything, Ice," she whispers, licking her lips as she cups my dick through my jeans.

Tanya, or whatever her name is, rolls up on to her toes to lick at my neck. I take a glance at my watch. Although someone could walk in, even if it is too early for the club to open, I should have enough time for a quick fuck before most people start arriving.

"Then go down," I command.

Without a word, Tanya drops to her knees before she unsnaps and unzips my jeans without hesitation. Her soft hands grip my semi-hard cock and stroke gently, stirring it to life.

Tanya is a curvy girl, with an amazing hourglass figure. Her tits are far more than a mouthful or handful. Her ass is made for slapping, her legs tone like a dancer's with thighs made to grip. Her long, dark hair flows down her back in waves.

All thoughts escape me as her velvet soft tongue runs up the length of my shaft. When her lips wrap around my now painfully hard dick, I grab her head and pull her to me, forcing my cock deep down her throat. She freezes, getting her gag reflex under control, before she starts sucking hard, hollowing out her cheeks.

"That's right, take it," I growl.

She keeps sucking then dragging her teeth gently across my now fully throbbing erection as she pulls her head back. Her tongue swirls around the head before she engulfs me yet again, her lips sliding down the length.

Her head bobs up and down in a steady pace as she continues to lick, suck, and stroke me.

Cupping my balls, she squeezes them, and my body goes tight as I hold her head still and shoot my come down her throat. When I feel her struggle to swallow, I release her head and pull out. My seed spills out of the corner of her mouth, and she reaches up to wipe it as the last drops fall from my cock, shamelessly onto her shirt.

Stuffing myself back into my jeans, I am about to walk away when her tiny hand reaches up to grab my wrist.

"What?" I bark out. It should be obvious I am done with her. With our history, she should know I don't coddle. I don't cuddle, and I damn sure don't hold conversations. Right now, I don't have time, so I won't be fucking her. Why is she still here, much less trying to talk to me? "I'm done, Tammy. Got shit to do, so you can go."

Rising from her knees, my cum still on her shirt, her eyes plead with me, although for what exactly, I am unsure. "I need a job. And my name is Tally."

"We fucked a handful of times before, and you're a good piece of ass. You suck cock like a damn pro. If I hire you, I can't fuck you."

"I need a job, Ice."

"So you thought you'd get down on your knees or on your back? There is a job title for that, and it's not a stripper. Get the fuck outta here and don't come back."

Walking away, I don't bother to look back, even when I hear the whimpering of her crying behind me. We sell pussy, but the girls we have for that don't earn that place with their bodies. It is an agreement they have, and it is not one earned by freely giving out the merchandise. Yeah, I am one fucking cold-hearted bastard. Tell me something I don't already know.

Morgan

Pulling up to my parent's house, I take a deep breath. One day, I will learn to say no. One day, I will not answer their summons. One day, I will be free of their hold.

Too bad my parents spent so much time drilling their rules into me and not my younger sisters. Madyson is untamed and reckless. She thinks she is invincible, that nothing will touch her. Whereas Mallory is more reserved, emotional, dark, and brooding. I think my youngest sister faces a serious need for attention, or she is dealing with teen depression. She wears all black, all the time. Her eyebrow piercing, her nose piercing, and the one she has above her lip she calls a Monroe piercing were all done by her friend in her bedroom. She is only fourteen; why put holes in your body while so young?

Getting out of my car, I walk up the curved sidewalk lined with a variety of flowers and Hosta plants. I know, without looking, that the brightly colored garden extends to across the front of the house and around to the back where my mother keeps a large, pristine garden to entertain guests in. The sight of the well-maintained

29

flowers only serves to make me angry since I know she pays the gardener a fortune to keep up the numerous plants. It is money they don't really have since they are drowning in debt, due to gratuitous spending on an almost lavish lifestyle they can't afford yet feel like they need. Heck, they can't afford this gaudy, over-sized house. Will they sell it and move into something more affordable, though? No.

I pause as I open the six thousand dollar mahogany door with a decorative window. Staring at the Victorian design in the glass, I think about making a run for it. I don't want to be here, but if I defy their summons, I know my parents will take it out on my sisters. They have it hard enough; I don't need to make it worse for them.

Walking in, the nostalgia one should feel when coming home fails to wash over me. While I take my shoes off at the front door, as I have been trained to do, I pause to take in my childhood home.

Mahogany wood flooring runs throughout the house and is covered here and there in lavish Turkish rugs. To my right is the formal sitting room where an antique settee, chaise, and wingback chair sit facing each other in front of an ornate fireplace. Seeing that stupid chaise brings back bad memories of my mother teaching me how a 'lady' lounges on one.

Ignoring the staircase to my left that would lead me to my sister's bedrooms, as well as my old room, I move down the front hall. The walls are not covered in family photos or anything else that would showcase a parent's love for their children. No, instead, there are large oil paintings of foxhunts and carriage rides through old

English cities. The few family pictures that are present are staged for one to grab a quick look and move on to something else.

The hallway leads me to the living room, which looks much the same as the formal sitting room. Over on the side of the room, I see a new, opulent, antique console table with a white marble top. I don't want to know how many thousands of dollars that cost my father. What is apparent is that my mother is still living well beyond her means, as if she were married to a cardiac surgeon instead of the family dentist my father is.

Blowing out a deep breath, I plaster on a fake smile and get ready to face the lion's den. It is all about appearances. Fake it until you make it back out the door.

Walking into the formal dining room, I see my father is already seated at the head of the table, reading a newspaper, as my mother sets a large pot roast down. Noticeably absent are both of my sisters, meaning I will be facing my parents alone. Great.

I politely greet both of them before my father waves me to the chair next to him. Do either of my parents bother to get up and give me a hug or kiss on the cheek? No. God forbid they actually show their children any affection. What would the neighbors think? We wouldn't want old Mrs. Ackerman telling everyone they coddled their girls.

Sitting down to dinner, I am still waiting to be informed of why my presence has been requested. They summoned, I came; why can't we get on with it? Why such a charade?

"How are you, Morgan?" my slightly balding father asks me, aiming for casual conversation.

"Fine, sir," I answer, deciding to keep my answers short to try to get through this evening quicker. However, I must not forget to address them with manners. To fail to do so would end up in a lecture an hour long about how I should always respect my elders.

"We've asked you to come because your cousin, Sarah, is getting married in three weeks. Mallory and Madyson can't attend, so you must go with us," my mother informs me.

Unable to hide the shock on my face, I momentarily sit with my mouth wide open. My sisters choose this moment to enter the room without a greeting. Rather than wait for my brain to catch up and give a reply, my sister, Madyson, wades into the conversation.

"Seriously, why does Morgan need to go? You could go by yourselves, you know. For whatever reason, you won't be seen with Mallory or me, but you'll torture Morgan by making her sit through Sarah's wedding. Warped. Y'all are completely warped."

"We are family, a close family," my mom annunciates each word. "Weddings are family events. Therefore, we are expected to arrive as a family. I can explain Madyson and Mallory have school commitments and are unable to attend, but we need you there to show we are a cohesive unit, Morgan."

"Mallory and I are available to go, but you won't let us," Madyson continues her argument that it should be them, not me, attending.

Quite frankly, I don't see why any of us need to go the wedding of a cousin we haven't spoken to in years. However, my parents will never agree with that sentiment. It all boils down to the dog and pony show they demand I put on for our family. It is about appearances, after all. We couldn't have the rest of the Powell clan thinking our little family unit was anything less than perfect.

"Look at you!" my dad snaps as he waves his hand at Madyson's short denim skirt and tank top. "Half the time you prance around like a little whore. Not to mention you act as though you have no respect, whatsoever, for your elders. Your sister is a freak-show. She sulks around the house, listening to that god-awful screeching she calls music while putting more holes in her face. There is no way we are taking either of you to a family event." His voice is condescending, though rife with authority, to let his middle daughter know this is the end of the conversation. His blunt, nasty summarization of both of my younger sisters is all he needs for both him, and our mother, to justify their heartless attitudes and ridiculous request of me.

"Where did we go wrong?" he snidely asks his wife.

"I don't know… hmmm… maybe spending all your energy making sure Morgan was the perfect child while completely ignoring us," Madyson quips.

"Madyson Leigh Powell, that's enough of your disrespect! If you followed the rules and acted appropriately, you would be able to go with us. Instead, you're always like a ticking time bomb, waiting to go off or doing something stupid like flashing your rear end in those scraps of fabric you call skirts to men twice your age. We can't trust you to not make us look bad. We have three girls. At least one of you needs to be with us, and it needs to be Morgan," my mother states, slamming her fork down to make it clear there will be no further discussion on the topic.

Madyson starts to chime in again when I put my hand up to stop her. She is fighting a losing battle. It is better for everyone involved if I simply go and get it done with.

"See, at least one of you is agreeable. Oh, and Morgan, you will need to bring a date. People are beginning to wonder if you have"—she leans in towards me—"deficiencies" —she leans back again—"since you never have a boyfriend. Sarah is younger than you; thus, we need to show everyone you will be the next one to get married."

I only nod my head in agreement. Why must everything be about what people see or think?

Chapter

4

Ice

"Sandoval."

"Ice, good to see you handling this trade personally. I have much respect for a man who stays so intimately involved in his business." His heavy Cuban accent laces each word.

Lazaro Sandoval stands before me, a true 'Don.' The tailor made, gray pinstriped suit covers a pastel pink button down shirt that only further highlights his tan skin, his jet black hair gelled back to perfection. My six foot frame towers over the man, although his short stature does nothing to make his presence any less intimidating. No, this man is contained fury. His venom runs right below the surface, waiting for a reason to be released. He would be as deadly as they come, except I am deadlier. So is every man in my club. He simply hasn't realized it yet.

Lazaro Sandoval has earned his title one kill at a time. Each territory he controls has been acquired meticulously, with his very own hands. He doesn't keep an enforcer on his team. It is his thrill to personally see to ending his opponent when he has been crossed. This is a man who is not afraid to get dirty, not in the least bit.

"If you want something done right, do it yourself, or so they say," I state, making sure my voice shows I am far from being intimidated by him. Others may cower in his presence, but to me, he is nothing more than another scumbag I have every intention of burying. I merely have to wait for the right time, gather all my evidence, and worm out the information from him that my boys and I need to know.

"They would be correct," Lazaro agrees, a creepy smile spreading across his face. "You know, a man in my position can't be too safe. A man like me doesn't get where he's at by doing business with just any yuma for quick money."

"No, a bisñero, such as yourself, can't do business with any foreigner, as you say. Funny you call me the foreigner here, though. Last time I checked, it's my country you live in, not your own." I am possibly pushing my luck here, but this smug fucker needs to remember where he is.

"Ice," my name rolls off his tongue in a hiss, "understand that one in my position must learn of their allies and adversaries. A man of my power must also treat my allies as my future enemy."

My blood boils as I fight to maintain composure. The man before me easily dishes out threats as if they are compliments.

"This is a simple business transaction, Sandoval. Certainly you can understand the concept of supply and demand. You have a supply for a product in demand, one in which I wish to purchase. Consider me your frienemy, that's fine by me, but let's cut the bullshit and handle business."

He laughs at me, rubbing his hands together. "Impatience can be a weakness, Ice. Being too quick for one's release could cost you relationships, both personally and professionally. A woman wants a man with stamina and endurance. Both are key traits in business and the bedroom. Trusting one with a product, as well cut as mine, is much like sharing a woman. A beauty writhing under you makes it hard to control your load. Releasing too soon promises the lady will not return. You are far from a teenage boy unable to control his dick. As a man with much experience and control, with both women and business, I will dispense half of what you have requested. Once my associates on the street confirm you handle your street business with as much discretion as you do your club business, we will renegotiate the terms of our partnership."

This smug bastard is pushing my buttons just to fuck with me. He has already scouted every avenue of our businesses. I know because I let the information be fed to him so we could move forward with our deal. At this point, he knows everything there is to be found about the Regulators. It took months to even get a meeting with the man to negotiate any sort of affiliation. He is more than patient, more than thorough, and more than on his game.

Hammer shifts behind me, feeling my agitation.

"Time is money, Sandoval. You know this. With such an ego about your blanca, I need a sample before this goes any further. You stand here, changing the terms of our agreement by only releasing half of my order, yet the powder I seek may be nothing more than angel dust."

With the sharp raise of his arm, his pointer finger going up, one of his men shifts and turns back to the car from which they exited. We are in a private hangar used by many Cubans who are transporting goods from South Beach back to their communities in small cargo planes. My intel states the hangar is owned by a prominent plastic surgeon in downtown Miami.

From what we have gathered, Sandoval is not bringing the drugs in via planes, though we haven't worked out his system yet. It has taken months of build-up along with multiple negotiations and shows of good faith before we could get him to do any business with us. After a few small transactions with his low ranking men and lower cost products, we have finally gotten into larger opportunities.

His man makes his way back over to me, carrying with him a small brick of white powder ready to be cut and distributed. The drug has the street value of gold that I need in my club's possession like yesterday. He hands the cocaine over to Sandoval, who extends the brick to me, smiling cryptically. I can read him. He is testing me. All future transactions will rely on how I react to the drugs.

Taking the package, I pull out my pocket knife. Having been stripped of our guns and knives entering the building, I am lucky to have kept this. If these men only knew what I could do with this two inch blade if pushed to my limits. Fuckers. Hell, I don't need a small knife to kill the man if I wanted to; I could do that with my bare hands.

Slicing the package open, I dip the tip of my knife in. I scoop up only the slightest amount then lift it to my nose and inhale. The burn in my nasal passages is hard to stand, my eyes immediately glaze over in unshed tears.

"Sandoval, you have good reason to be cocky," I state, letting him know I am impressed with his product.

He laughs at me. The man stands before me and laughs as if he has not one care in the world. If I get my way, he is going to have a shitload of stuff to worry about, including keeping his own useless hide alive.

"I like you very much, Ice. It's refreshing to find a biker that won't use more of my product than he sells. From your reaction, I can tell that you are not a user. This tells me the Regulators will go far in this business. Nothing irritates me more than someone being held back by chemical dependencies. I have found men tend to become weak to their addictions, whether that be the pussy in their bed, the drugs in their bodies, or the money in their wallets. You do not strike me as a man with weaknesses; I foresee a long and profitable future for us both."

With the confirmation of his approval, his men shift and begin unloading black crate, after black crate from a nearby SUV. Placing the boxes in front of us, each one is opened for our inspection before being closed and passed off to Hammer. Then he and three other patched Regulators load the crates into our waiting van.

Bending down to my feet, I pick up the duffle bag of cash. I open it and remove five stacks of bills, tossing them over to Coal to put back in the van.

"Since you adjusted the amount of our product, I've adjusted the amount of your pay." Passing the bag to him, I continue, "Understand, Sandoval, I'm not a man of patience. I'm not a man of mercy. And I sure as shit am not a man who plays games. This is the only leniency I'll allow you since we are still getting to know one another. I understand a man of your position has to protect himself, just like a man of my authority does. Luckily, for us both, I do not sell products I don't already have in my possession. That way, I won't have a disappointed buyer. We both know what that could do."

"You are a worthy business associate. I'm sure we will have a mutually beneficial future together," Sandoval replies as he backs away, not removing his eyes from me until reaching his vehicle.

I realize now that I have underestimated him. He is a cocky fucker, yet smart. Never trust your men to truly have your back when your murder could give them an empire that would make them richer than their wildest dreams.

After he is pulling away in his vehicle we make our way to the bikes and waiting van. Getting on my Harley, I nod to Hammer who will take the van and handle the drugs we have purchased. The knot in my stomach eases knowing we have made another step deeper into the world of Lazaro Sandoval and the Cuban Mafia.

It is also one step closer to ending a man who needs to be taken out for good.

It is going to take a lot of diligence from both me and my men to get the information we need to take Sandoval out without backlash on the Regulators. There is a delicate balance between what we let the world see and what everyone has no clue we have going on in the background. We can't afford to be exposed in any way. It would put us all in danger from more underground players than we could point an M-16 at. With each passing day that I have to deal with Sandoval, I see the man is too deadly to let live.

At least I am getting paid good money to kill him.

Morgan

No. no. no.

Coming down the sidewalk, after picking up my morning latte, my heel gets stuck in the crack of two concrete rectangles. When I attempt to pull it out, the heel comes unglued from the shoe. Now, every step I take, it flaps and makes walking awkward. I was on schedule, but the barista was slow and apparently new; as a result, my regular skinny caramel treat took longer than usual. Add my newest mishap, and I am officially ten minutes late for work.

I am never late.

No, being late would be falling short. I never fall short. People depend on me. I have a commitment to arrive at work at nine sharp, not ten minutes after. I get paid to be on time and in dress code, which I am sure doesn't include broken shoes.

Monday mayhem welcomes me with open arms. After the weekend stock changes, I will need to smooth over the fears of some of my clients, as well as convince others that now is the time to transition a portion of their funds. My mind dances with numbers, stock names, and racing thoughts of multiple accounts muddle together as I enter the bank.

"Morgan," I hear my coworker, Aimee, call out.

Looking over my shoulder to her while still walking, I miss the extremely tall, bald man wearing all black, including a black leather vest as he turns and bumps into me harshly. My latte sloshes, spilling out of my cup and over both of us. I gasp in surprise as I look up at the overly intimidating man.

"Oh my, I am so sorry," I stammer as I stumble on my broken shoe to get distance between us.

"Pay attention. Quit tryin' to be cute, and look where you're goin'."

What is it with the men I meet lately being assholes?

"Excuse me," I reply, looking at the patches on his vest. 'Coal' lays over the left side of his vest, right at his heart. 'Vice President' lays on his right side. Across the rest, I see different patches with different cities and sayings.

Deciding I need to smooth this over for multiple reasons, I fidget nervously. I need to defuse this situation because this man scares the bejesus out of me. Yet I find him attractive, and this confuses me. The second reason I need to calm down is this is my job, and the third being I wasn't paying attention; therefore, this is my fault.

"My apologies, mister… Sorry, I don't know your name. I apologize for not looking where I was going, and I promise you I wasn't trying to be cute," I manage to get out weakly.

"Coal. Name is Coal." His temperament softens as he lifts his hand and proceeds to lick the remnants of my morning addiction off him. Leaning down, he whispers in my ear, "You don't have to try to be cute; it's just you."

My breath hitches as I feel him breathing down my exposed neck. God, it is hot in here. Asshole or not, this man screams sex. Suddenly, I wish I had worn my hair down today rather than in the extremely tight bun it is currently stuck in.

"Definitely cute and definitely just you. Innocence is a rare thing. Keep it safe." The last words come out while he pulls away, meeting my gaze as his eyes darken with an emotion I can't read.

He is gone before I can gather my composure and move on to my office. I don't even get to clean myself up before Aimee is hot on my heels.

"Oh, my God! He actually spoke to you."

"Huh?" I question absentmindedly, not having a clue what she is talking about.

"Trevor Blake. He comes in every third Monday of the month and doesn't ever speak to anyone but Joshua. He won't let anyone else help him. He's part of the

Regulators Motorcycle Club. That's why I called your name."

"Why would you call my name in reference to him?" I ask her, confused.

"To get his attention, hello."

"How does calling my name get his attention exactly?" I don't understand why women do stuff like this. Is it really that difficult to talk to a man? Granted, I have never tried, but seriously, I don't get it.

"You were right there beside him. Therefore, calling your name, he would follow your gaze and see me." She reaches up and squeezes her own perky and very fake breasts. "And my rack is rockin' today. I'm wearing my new push up bra. It would be a perfect day for him to notice me."

I have no response for her. None. I am baffled that anyone would do this for the simple attention of a man. I also don't get why a woman who has fake breasts so large they barely move, would wear a push up bra to accentuate what is already perky and in your face. Thankfully my phone ringing saves me from more of her nonsense. She adds a quick goodbye and leaves as I take off to enter my office.

Leaning over my desk, my already tight suit skirt pulls snugly against my curves as I stretch for my phone. "Morgan Powell," I greet after picking up the bulky receiver and sitting my half empty latte on my desk.

"Can you pick me up after school?" my sister Madyson asks from the other end.

"What?" I shriek. "I do not have time for this, Madyson."

"Mom and Dad have kicked me out. They took my car and everything. I need somewhere to stay and a ride. I thought I would be able to stay with Brooke, but her dad needs a damn security clearance before she can have a house guest. Please, Morgan, I don't have anywhere to go. It will only be a few days until Mom cools off."

Knowing how my parents are, they have probably decided, since she is eighteen, they can kick her out. They know she has no college aspirations or at least any she has shared. With her behavior it saves them money as they would want to pay for her education as they did mine. Reality is, they can't afford it. Her unwillingness to mold into the person they want her to be only adds to the division between them. Besides, if they make her leave, they don't have to cover up what a disobedient child they have to their friends and neighbors.

"How is any of this my problem?" I harshly question. She could try to get along with them, at least for the sake of having a roof over her head, until she finishes school; but no, not my sister. Does she think I enjoyed growing up with them, having their absurd rules and expectations shoved down my throat? I did what I had to until I could afford to live on my own.

"It's not, but I have no one else," she pleads, tugging at my heartstrings.

A knock at my office's door jamb has me turning around to see my boss staring at me with an odd expression. This is going to be the never ending morning of crazy.

Making a quick decision I know I will regret, though at the moment my options are limited, I turn my attention back to my sister. "I'm sorry, I gotta go, Madyson." Hearing her sob into the phone, I realize things may be more serious than I first assumed. Madyson is a lot of things, but a crier is not one of them, when it comes to our parents. Before I give it a second thought, I relent. "Can you get a ride to my apartment? You can stay until this blows over."

"Thank you," she whispers, trying to get her crying under control.

She hangs up as I do, and then I turn to face the man whose gaze is burning into my backside.

"Mr. Walton," I greet, putting on the fake smile my mother taught me to perfection.

"I noticed you hadn't logged into your email yet, just checking to see if you were in."

Feeling insecure as my supervisor stands there, taking me in, I reach down to smooth out my skirt, to realize my arm is sticky from my run in with the Coal guy. My broken shoe, stained suit jacket, sticky arm, and personal phone call all add up to show him just what a truly inept employee he has.

"I'm sorry," I say lamely.

"We have our weekly assignments meeting at ten today, instead of nine-thirty. See you there, Miss Powell."

The rest of my day passes in a blur of one mishap after another. The printer decided to eat my sales report. While trying to unjam the caught papers, I popped the wrong little spring, rendering the whole thing useless. Lunch should have been safe, yet one distraction and ketchup dropped directly on my white shirt, dead center of my boobs, equaled me becoming a target for attention all day long. Why yes, world, please stare at my boobs. Unfortunately, I am not Aimee with her fake breasts. Having a man look at me below eye level is utterly unnerving.

After spending as much time as I can hiding my feet under my desk to avoid having to wear the broken shoe, I face the flapping heel once more to make my way to my car. All should have been well, but alas, it is not. My keyless remote fails. Fumbling with my keys, I scratch the doors of my little sedan, and my heel gives out again, causing my ankle to roll and me to fall to the pavement below. This is the endless day of crap.

I get home, walking up to my doorstep, barefoot and limping, and there sits Madyson, head on her knees, quiet. One thing my sister is not would be quiet. When I unlock my door, she doesn't move.

"Madyson, come on."

Following me inside, she carries her backpack and a duffle bag. I head into my kitchen to fix a frozen pizza for dinner. I don't have much, but she shouldn't be here long. We can make do. I look over at her and take in her swollen eyes, red cheeks, and defeated demeanor.

"You wanna talk about it?" I ask gently.

"Nothing to talk about. I took Mallory to the free clinic to get birth control. Mom found out. She freaked and said I ruined Mal. They kicked me out, took my car and cell phone, and then they gave me my birth certificate and social security card before they sent me away. I walked to school. I called you from the school office. They had a phone book for me to find your office number. I couldn't remember your cell since it was programmed in my phone."

"Give it time, Madyson. They'll come around," I tell her, even though I am not fully convinced myself. At this point, I can only hope they will come around. Otherwise, what am I supposed to do with her? I barely made it out of my own teenager years with my sanity intact because of our parents. Me trying to reign in all that is my little sister might be enough to finally put me in a nuthouse.

Chapter

5

Ice

Three weeks later...

"How many are we at right now?" I question the men in front of me. Every patched member of the Regulators MC sits here, all of us going over the details of yet another missing woman.

"Twelve in our zip code. Sixty-eight in our territory," Coal answers.

"That's fuckin' twelve too many at our back door!" I shout, feeling out of control.

"We can't hire them all. We can't hide them all," Hammer states the obvious.

"No, we can't, but we can shut this shit down. According to Commander Wall and his team, Medina named Lazaro Sandoval as the ring leader. Why can't we tie him to the missing girls? Where the fuck is he keeping them?"

"All questions we are trying to get answers to," Coal glares at me.

"Why do I have more fuckin' questions than answers? Riddle me that, knuckleheads. We do not exist.

We are not who any of these scum bags think we are. We have resources above and beyond any alphabet agency in this country can access, and you all sit in here and tell me there is yet another girl missing in our territory. All of this, and we have no new information?"

"We're working on it as much as we can without drawing attention. Sandoval has his stuff locked tight, Ice," Screech pipes in.

"So unlock it," I snarl back.

"Fuck you," Coal narrows his eyes. "It's not that simple, and you damn well know it. Get laid, go for a run, blow something the fuck up—I don't care what you do, but don't sit here and make it sound so simple."

I won't take shit from many people, but Coal has made a valid point. We have been buying drugs consistently from Sandoval. We have built the foundation of a strong affiliation with him. However, it hasn't been enough.

"Time to step up our ties to Sandoval. We buy guns next, work our way in. We may have to buy the pussy to find his inner workings, but in the meantime, we need to get our people in every damn club we can. The more eyes we have, the closer we can come to stopping the next target from becoming a victim."

"Agreed," Hammer begins yet is cut off by my phone ringing.

Without looking at the screen, we all know it is Brooke calling based on the set ring tone.

"In the middle of something, baby girl," I answer in the hopes of deterring her from going on with teenage ramblings.

She is supposed to be spending the night at her friend Madyson's house, who did check out, finally, from Screech's report. The girl has a three point eight grade point average and takes two honors classes with Brooke. She may come off as a rebellious punk-ass teen, but she actually has two partial scholarships to college based on her grades in math alone.

Madyson Powell's sister, Morgan, is more clean-cut than any twenty-four-year-old should be. According to the reports on her, I doubt she has ever had a single drink. I had guys watch both Powell sisters for two weeks before I agreed to let Brooke spend the night there. Things aren't always what they seem. I know that better than anyone.

At first glance, I assumed Morgan was irresponsible with her younger sister. It turns out she was merely adjusting as her sister made the choice to live with her instead of their parents. This made me curious as to why an eighteen-year-old would make a decision like that, so I had Screech dig into their parents next. After looking over the reports, the debt and overall character information we were able to obtain, their parents wouldn't be a place I would want to grow up in or have Brooke around. They are more focused on keeping up with the Jones', so to speak, than being a real family.

My thoughts are shaken when Brooke whispers into the phone, "Come get us, Daddy."

My stomach drops, my heart stops, and everything ceases to exist around me. "Where are you, and what the fuck is goin' on?"

"It's… it's… it's Madyson. We're at a party. They slipped her something, and I can't get her to wake up enough to get her out of the house."

"Don't drink anything, not even water. Don't move. I'm gonna give the phone to Screech. He will get the address and get it to Hammer. We're coming right now. You don't hang up that phone; you stay on the line with Screech until you see me and I end your call."

I don't bother explaining shit to anyone. Screech will get the information I need and get it to my brother. I hand him my phone as I point to Hammer and then the door. Then I signal for Coal to continue the meeting and try to see if we are missing anything.

Running out of the building, I hop in my truck. Hammer follows suit, not climbing on his bike. If Madyson is as bad as Brooke says, there is no way it's safe for her to ride.

Pulling up to yet another obnoxiously large house, with cars parked everywhere in front of it, I get out of my truck. Only, this time, I don't have to look for my daughter. Instead, I find her on the front porch, holding her friend close to her side. When she sees me, she drops Madyson without thinking and runs towards me. Madyson slumps over slowly, falling onto the porch. Brooke hugs me tight, and I can feel the wetness on her cheeks from crying.

"Daddy," she whispers, gripping me tighter and crushing me a little more inside.

My mind drifts back to the first time I held her. I thought for sure I would drop her or let her down. I wanted to run, to hide, to scream, and hell, cry. I was a barely eighteen-year-old dipshit, scared shitless of something that weighed six pounds. Then her eyes struggled to blink, but they opened. Slowly but surely, she looked at me and saw straight into my soul. I would never drop her, I would never let her down, and I damn sure would never let her go. For in those baby blue eyes was my entire being looking back at me. Nothing in my entire life will ever compare to having her.

Holding her close, I watch as Hammer effortlessly scoops up an incoherent Madyson to carry her to the truck. I then nod at him and pull away from Brooke to look down at her. In this moment, my teenage daughter doesn't look like the young woman she is growing into. No, right now she looks like she did when she was seven, and I took the training wheels off her bicycle—scared out of her mind. Yes, baby girl, this too is unchartered territory for us.

"Brooke—" I start, but she puts up her hand to stop me.

"I'm sorry, Daddy. You were right about everything. We snuck out, and we shouldn't have. I didn't think anyone would actually do anything to us. It was supposed to be a good time. Daddy, I'm worried about Madyson," she whimpers.

"Let's go."

It was time to teach Morgan Powell, once and for all, that she needed to step up and take better care of her sister.

Morgan

"Morgan, you are beautiful," he whispers in my ear before he kisses down my neck then licks the sensitive curve where it meets my shoulder.

My body is hot with need. The demand burning deep. With my arms bound above my head by his tie, I lie spread before him, naked as the day I was born, nothing held back. He kisses his way down between my breasts, the gruff feeling of his five o'clock shadow scraping my overly sensitive flesh.

I wiggle underneath him, seeking more contact, more everything.

I feel his hands slide up my inner thighs while he begins to give attention to my breasts. The tingle inside me builds. Anticipation.

Ring.

What is ringing? There shouldn't be any ringing here. My dream man wouldn't dare bring anything that would distract him from his time with me. Shaking my head, I slowly open my eyes. He is gone. There is no tie. I am in my bed, in my dark room, alone. Completely alone.

Always alone.

Turning my head, I see my phone lighting up on my nightstand. The time on my alarm clock reads a little after midnight. Grabbing the annoying dream-interrupting device, I slide it over to answer without looking at the caller ID.

"Hello," I manage to answer, though I am unable to hide the sleep in my voice.

"You would think, when you have someone else's kid at your place, you would, I don't know, stay the fuck awake until they go to sleep."

"Huh, who is this?" I ask, suddenly very confused.

"Brooke's dad. I had to go pick up my daughter and your sister tonight, while you were counting sheep."

Oh, no, no, no! I thought she was doing better. We had a long talk about the fact that I can't be worrying over her and this rebellious stage. I need to focus on work and providing for us. Since she has been here for a few weeks, without giving me any problems, I never thought she and her friend would sneak out. Heck, I baked cookies with them tonight before bed. We did face masks, painted nails, and all that teenage girl sleepover stuff.

Brooke seemed like a nice enough girl, making me feel like they would behave. How did they leave? Why did they leave?

"Are they okay?" I ask as my anxiety rises.

"No," he barks out at me.

Tears pool behind my eyes. My sister is misunderstood. She has lived her entire life in my shadow with impossible parents who have unrealistic expectations. Not only have I failed her, but now Brooke, too.

"Get your ass over to my house. Madyson was slipped something. I have my doctor coming over to check her out, but she is gonna want you when she starts comin' around." Before I can reply, he disconnects the call.

Well, asshole, I would come over, but I don't know where you live. My phone pings with a text of his address and gate code before I can let my thoughts further consume me.

Pulling up to the house, I see it is far from modest. Not as big as my parents yet certainly more welcoming. First impressions would say this is a family home. I would envision a businessman in a suit living here, a far cry from what I know I will find.

When I reach the front door, I don't even have to ring the bell as the door is opened by another guy in a leather vest I have never seen before. His strong jawline and stern face let me know he is not the welcoming committee.

"Hammer, send her back. No time for her to ogle the damn house," I hear the voice of my nightmares yell out.

I roll my eyes, and the guy who is apparently Hammer smiles at me. "I wouldn't do that around Ice if I were you."

"Who is Ice?" I find myself asking in a whisper. I met the guy with the patch 'Ice' briefly the night he dropped Madyson off, but I am not sure who he is exactly.

"Brooke's dad. He doesn't much like it when she rolls her eyes. As cute as you are, he won't take that shit from you, either."

Involuntarily, I roll my eyes again. This causes Hammer to laugh, and for some reason, it relaxes me. He is a guy I am sure I should be seriously afraid of, but in this moment, my fears and insecurities are wrapped up in a dad that goes by the name of Ice. Shaking my head, I try to push aside all my thoughts while I follow Hammer inside to find my sister.

"How is Madyson? What happened? They were in bed when I went to my room, I swear," I ask frantically as I make my way farther into the house.

"She was roofied at a party they apparently snuck out and went to. We got the doc to check her out. It has to pass through her system. She's gonna feel like shit for the next day or so, but no long term effects. Brooke knew something was wrong and called her dad, and we went and picked them up. Follow me, they're back in the guest suite."

The sounds coming from the room let me know someone is seriously sick. *Oh, Madyson, what did you get yourself into?*

Entering the room, it is something from a magazine or an advertisement. The room that Hammer called the guest suite on the bottom floor gives off an upscale hotel feel rather than the cozy comforts of home vibe. My sister is lying in a bed, puking into a trashcan that Brooke is holding while visibly trying not to puke herself. The sight would be funny if the situation were not so serious.

"Yack it up. Remember every fucking minute of this. When you two think of pulling some shit like this again, remember tonight. Remember the fear, remember the sickness, and remember the punishment," Ice is barking out at the two girls. "Because this is far from over. You both are grounded. I don't give a shit if you aren't mine, Madyson. Your sister obviously isn't equipped to tackle you, so I'm gonna handle it for her."

"Excuse me," I interrupt sharply. "How about I talk to the girls to find out what happened? Then I can determine an appropriate punishment."

"Or how about you sit your pretty little ass on the other side of that bed with your sister and let me make sure these two think twice before they do this again?"

"I'm sure they get the point, and they will get it a lot clearer after we've all had some rest and recovered. You can preach to them all you want after my sister is able to keep a meal down; deal, papa bear?"

"Awe, look at you being all cute," he states sarcastically as his dark brown eyes glittering with rage, stares me down, trying to intimidate me.

Honestly, I want to run and hide in a closet because the guy could totally squash me. However, there is something about him that makes me want to challenge him. Maybe because he is a complete jackass every single time I have had to deal with him, or maybe he brings that out in everyone. I don't know, but I don't plan on putting up with his attitude much longer.

"Daddy, please. Yell at me tomorrow, but don't be mad at Morgan. She didn't know we had plans. Hell, we didn't even have a car. She seriously thought we were asleep. Mady and I have learned our lesson, but you can teach us more tomorrow if you will be nice to Morgan." Her teenage eyes tear up as she defends me.

Ice stares silently at his daughter for what feels like hours yet is really only seconds. Then he glances over to me as my sister moans when she sits up to find me.

"I'm sorry, Morgan," Madyson whispers as tears freely flow down her face when her eyes finally find mine.

My poor little sister is hurting. There is so much here that Ice doesn't know. There is a pain in her eyes that goes far beyond her being drugged tonight. I don't care what this man says; I do know how to handle my sister. I didn't see it before, but she needs me. She needs understanding and, most of all, someone to give her unconditional love. I have spent my whole life being what my parents wanted me to be for my sisters, whereas I should have been more of a sister instead of trying to be their savior while I was there.

From this night forward, that is what she and Mallory will have from me. The sister they deserve, the support system they need, and the love they deserve.

ICE

Chapter
6

Ice

Drama, drama, drama. It is always some sort of drama with the new girls at After Midnight. Someone took someone else's shit. Why did Suzie fuckin' Sunshine make headliner when I didn't, and my boobs are bigger? What do you mean I can't suck his cock during a VIP dance?

Aggravating bitches.

In my mind, it is simple—dance. They get paid to dance, nothing more, nothing less. Why can't they be like the guys over at Alibi? Very rarely do we have issues amongst them. It seems like every time we get a new girl, there has to be some sort of drama for a bit until everyone settles back down.

My head is pounding. I have spent the last hour listening to the cat fight coming out of the dressing room. I am two seconds from shoving a ball gag in both their mouths, chaining them to the poles, and burning all their shit. I guarantee they won't like my version of BDSM. There would be no pleasurable spankings and orgasms. Nope. In fact, I wouldn't touch them at all, but they would probably call me a sadist after they stared at the ashes of what used to be all of their expensive stage costumes.

The worst of the bunch, Ariana and Marisa, have been at each other over every little thing for three nights now. That is three nights too many, and I sure as shit won't listen to that nonsense for another three nights.

Add to my mind the thoughts continuing on a loop about Morgan and Madyson Powell, and I am in serious need of a punching bag or fresh pussy to pound out my frustrations.

Morgan spent two days at my house with her sister. Two days of agony as she had to wear my daughter's clothes—clothes that happened to be tight in all the right places—around me at every turn.

Madyson was miserable for about thirty-six hours. I hope she has been scared straight. Watching Madyson seemed to show Brooke I wasn't the warden holding her prisoner as much as I am a dad who doesn't want her hurt. I have already lost my wife; there is no way I would ever survive losing my baby girl, too.

I may have underestimated Morgan, though. She is a quiet, contained source of strength. Not once has she yelled, raised her voice, or cast judgment on her sister. Calmly, patiently, and lovingly, she has been there for her sister all the way. Her sister who, from what Brooke tells me, has been kicked out by her parents when I thought she had chosen to leave.

Is the teen girl a handful? Sure thing, but so is Brooke at times. From what I gather, her parents are not the supportive type. The family dynamic of their home is strange at best. According to Brooke, Madyson doesn't really have anyone, yet Morgan tries her best to be there for her. This situation seems to be bringing the siblings closer together.

Seeing the two sisters interact with each other has made me wonder. Does Brooke need more? Watching Morgan be there for Madyson is a stark reminder that all Brooke has is me and my brothers in the club. Parenthood is tough shit—the balance of letting go and holding on. I could survive in a desert without supplies for weeks easier than I can navigate my way through raising my daughter alone.

"Yo," Coal greets, entering my office and sitting on the couch in front of my desk.

Looking up, I meet the cold stare of a very pissed off, naturally brooding man. This is not good.

"Problem?" I question, knowing something serious has brought him in my office with that look.

"Crissy says she thinks we need to test some girls."

"Test some girls? Call the doc for pussy problems. I don't want to know anything that deals with what's between their legs. All I care about is that they're not giving their customers the sort of souvenirs that might broadcast what they've been up to. No one likes the gift that keeps on giving." Coal shakes his head, and I go alert. "We have a bigger issue on our hands?"

"Drug tests. She thinks it may extend beyond the stable," Coal states, not hiding his agitation.

Crissy is our After Midnight aunt, as she likes to call herself. She came to us four years ago, hooked on meth. Her mother pimped her out, starting at ten years old, to maintain her own habits. She was a skeleton covered in scars and sores when she literally stumbled into the wrong drug deal going very bad. Hammer saw her in the shadows and tried to stop her from coming out into the open, only she was too tweaked to see the slight shake of his head. When she came out, the overly anxious dealer panicked and pulled his piece on us. It is a kill or be killed world sometimes.

After that night, we sent Crissy to rehab, but she had nowhere to go when she got out. No plan, no escape, no world. That is a sure fire way to relapse; therefore, we took her in. Twice she has lost her footing and taken the hit, but currently she is nine hundred eighty-two days clean and completely sober. She doesn't drink, smoke cigarettes, or sell her pussy anymore. It has taken work, but she is solid. With her history, she can spot a user from a mile away.

"She would know. Set it up. If Crissy feels we need it, we need it. Hell, we probably need to do them more regularly anyway."

"It means she gets tested, too," Coal adds, watching me.

"She wouldn't call for a test if she was using."

"You don't think testing her will make her think we don't trust her? It could send her the wrong message, tempt her." Coal may be a bastard, but there is a heart in there somewhere. I think.

"Nah, she's solid. I wish I could say that for everyone else around us."

"I'll get it set up for first thing tomorrow morning."

We have a zero tolerance policy on drug use. The Regulators have a strict code for our members and employees. We provide a safe environment for people to come off the street and rebuild their lives. Crissy is one example. When she came to us, she had no job skills. We kept finding her selling sexual favors out on the street. That is a dangerous game to play. A John could get her in a situation and inject her with something, and she would be back to broken. If she was going to do it, we were going to keep her safe. That is how she came to work for us.

We don't keep a stable of hookers selling pussy like bets at a racetrack. There is no picking your top three contenders. Rather, we allow the women who wish to keep their sobriety on track, while rebuilding their lives, an opportunity to choose their clients, and we keep them safe while they handle their business. Instead of the John picking the girl, it is the girl picking her John. The agreement allows us to provide clean women to our associates while both the girls and Johns know the customers won't cross the lines set between them or face the wrath of my club.

The women in those beds are there by choice with the freedom to stop any time. Unfortunately, most of them have a background that doesn't leave them many options. Crissy has said many times she stays clean knowing, if she messes up, it is the door for her. I would hate to see that happen as the woman has shown nothing other than loyalty to my brothers and me. Rules are rules, though, and contrary to some people's thoughts, they aren't always meant to be broken.

Looking back to my paperwork, I sigh. It is always something around here. Dealing with bullshit has a way of making a man feel old before his time. Luckily, there is always a woman ready to spread her legs for me to make me feel young again.

Morgan

A month later…

"Oh, my God, what have you done?" I ask as I enter Brooke's kitchen to pick up Madyson.

"Ummm, hi, Morgan," my sister greets innocently. A little too innocently considering the sight in front of me.

The kitchen is a disaster. An entire container of flour must cover every inch of countertop and the floor. I see a bowl of what looks like an egg mixture, possibly with milk, sitting out on the counter with black specks floating in it. There are packages of cookies laid out across the table, the counter, and even one on the floor. The popping of the deep fryer scares me as I continue to take in the disaster before me.

"Do I want to know?" I ask, shaking my head at the two teens.

"Deep fried Oreos," Brooke pipes up cheerfully.

"What?" I laugh.

"We finished our homework early. I, like, don't ever cook. Grams taught me to bake, but we don't have the stuff. Mady said you love deep fried Oreos, so we thought we would make some for you and my dad."

"I take it this was not a successful endeavor, since I do not see batter covered goodies anywhere." Holding in my laughter is hard as I watch the seriousness of the girls' expressions.

"Neither of us knew what you are supposed to coat the cookies in," Madyson explains.

"Pancake batter," I say, smiling at their thoughtfulness.

"Oh, hell, why didn't we think of that?" Brooke rubs her hands on her very pink and extremely old lady apron.

"Come on, let's clean this up. I'll help you make dinner, and then we'll make a batch for dessert. For future reference, the internet is your friend."

Turning behind her, Brooke pulls out a yellow with lace trim apron and tosses it to me. I put the garment on and raise my eyebrow in question.

"Grams said, in order to be successful at something, you must first dress the part. If you walk in looking confident, you will become confident and therefore succeed, including cooking. So, we all have to look the part. Aprons on, hair pulled back, wash your hands, and make it happen," Brooke informs me confidently.

When she talks about her grandmother, her eyes dance in happy memories. I love the few times she has been around and shared with Madyson and me. Not having had these experiences, it is amazing to listen to.

Two hours later, the girls have helped me prepare a pasta bake for dinner and three packages of deep fried deliciousness. Just as I am emptying the last dish from the dishwasher, in walks the man of my nightmares. Okay, he is not really a nightmare, though he is far from a dream.

"What the fuck? You tryin' to move in because you can't afford the rent?" Ice greets coldly.

My stomach tightens, my palms sweat, and I want nothing more than to crawl in the oven and roast to avoid him. In the two days we stayed here, while Madyson recovered, he had not one nice thing to say to me. No, he spent the few times I did have to deal with him grilling me about my sister and giving advice on getting her under control. I thought for sure after that he wouldn't let Brooke hang out with her. However, he has made sure the girls have transportation after school to come to his house and do homework until I get off work to pick Mady up.

Since the day after Madyson recovered from being drugged, I have actually been able to go to work without worrying about what my sister would get into afterschool. In the month since, I have let the girls spend every afternoon here at Ice's house and every weekend with me. Granted, on those weekends, one of those bikers follows Brooke and hangs out in the parking lot of my complex. It is very unnerving to me, but at least Brooke is still allowed to be around Madyson.

Having Brooke around my sister is one of the best things I can give her. She is still reeling from my parents' abandonment. She might not admit it or talk to me about it, but I can tell being kicked out of their house has really shaken her up in ways that is staying with her. Seeing her haunted in such a way breaks my heart. I am determined to do everything I can to fill the parental role our crappy parents never tried to maintain.

Now I am worried this prick in front of me is going to compromise one of the few good things Madyson has going on in her life. I don't know what exactly I did to make him think I crapped in his Wheaties, but I have basically hit my breaking point with him. He is so sour he makes the Grinch pale in comparison.

"Daddy, Morgan cooked dinner. Don't be a dick," Brooke chastises with her hand on her hip.

"We were just leaving," I stammer.

"You should be gone. I'll play babysitter for your kid sister, but coming home to you in my kitchen is a no go. Don't let it happen again." He starts to turn away while my blood boils.

"Excuse me! No one asked you to play babysitter, protector, provider, or a damn thing." My sister gasps at my outburst as I take off the apron I am still wearing. "We are leaving, don't you fret about that. You won't find me in your kitchen again, either, so no worries there."

Tossing the apron on the counter, I hug Brooke quickly while Madyson is gathering her stuff. After pulling away, I watch as the man known as Ice stands completely still, taking me in. His gaze is so strong I feel like he is devouring me, and I am not completely sure he is doing it in a bad way.

I stomp past him, making sure to bump into him, and once I make it just beyond his reach, I turn back around. "Dinner is on the stove. Choke on the cookie when you eat it later, asshole," I add, feeling slightly crazed.

Chapter

7

Ice

One month later...

Three strippers were fired for popping positive on their drug tests. Crissy is on top of it. During our routine screens of the girls, we found one of the other girls is knocked up. I wish I could say the hiring process is the fun part of my job, but sadly it isn't; it is a constant fucking headache.

Hammer, Coal, and Skid sit in front of the main stage with me as we get ready to start auditions. The flooring around us is either black stained wood or a steel gray carpet, depending on where you are in the club. The walls are painted a soft dove gray, but to the casual observer, it would be hard to tell with the blue and purple neon lights everywhere. The comfortable black leather chair with silver studs allows me sit back so I am in a somewhat sprawled position and give off the façade that this audition is a waste of my time. It is our standard reception.

We give every woman who walks through our doors, looking for a job, the impression there is always something better to do than be in the same room with them. It is better to teach them from the get go that we don't have time for their bullshit.

As the petite bottle-blonde shifts her feet nervously on our main stage that runs across the back wall of our club, I feel my left eye twitch in irritation. The bright lights we use during cleaning are on instead of the dim, more sensual lighting used while the club is open. We need to be able to see the women and every flaw they may have if they are going to work here in any capacity.

One would be surprised how much dim overhead lights and bright neon colored lights along the stages can hide imperfections on a girl. No man wants to get hard for a woman dancing on the stage only to find out she is butt ugly when he waves her over for a private lap dance. At least, no sober man, that is. The drunk men probably don't care if a wrinkled up shrew is wiggling on their lap as long as they have beer googles on.

Sighing in boredom, I cross my foot over one leg as I look over to Hammer, who is tapping one of his boots on the black stained floors while he analyzes the woman in front of us. I am always thankful I have my brothers with me for this crap. It is good to have their opinions on the girls who can barely hold my attention. Not to mention, I have better shit to do than sit here for a woman who I am ninety percent sure won't be able to get a randy teenager hard with her dance. Still, our little After Midnight aunt seems adamant that we give the too tiny looking woman a chance. Fuck me, sometimes Crissy and her bleeding heart drive me nuts. We don't hire anyone that she doesn't find for us. Women try to get jobs by coming directly to us, but we want to know the story behind the body. Crissy does this and brings us the girls who need more than a job in the bigger picture of things.

Glancing back to the opposite end of the club, I think about getting myself a glass of whiskey. It might help me get through this nonsense. However, I know the boys and I have other shit to do today, the sort of work that requires a clear head and possibly my Glock if we end up in a bad spot.

Looking back at the woman who now looks like she is about to piss her little panties, due to all of the men staring at her, I decide to get this over with. I nod my head at Hammer, indicating for him to start.

"Name," Hammer barks out.

"Adalynn," the chick in front of us whispers.

"You want a job, step one is to actually speak. Time is money, don't waste ours."

She twists her hands nervously. It is evident this isn't her normal gig.

"Where did you come from?" Crissy recruits our auditions from other clubs or the streets. She finds the ones she thinks we can help the most.

"I've been working over at Titties and Tail."

"How's Mud treatin' you? What brings you here?" I ask. This is a make or break question before we take someone on when they have worked at another local club.

"He treats me fine. I was told I could make more money here, that's all," she once again whispers, making sure to avoid eye contact with all of us.

"That answer just saved your ass. Dance," Coal commands.

It is surprising how many times when asked how they are treated at their current or past employers they will spill all the secrets of the club. I happen to know, for a fact, Adalynn struggles at Titties. I also happen to know Mud has beaten her up pretty badly, twice, in the three months she has worked there. Doesn't matter what the girls look like at his club; no, all that matters is how good they suck and fuck.

Opening the file in front of me, I am surprised to find it empty. This further piques my interest in the fragile looking female. The music starts, and I can see her move in my peripheral vision, although I don't watch her dance. I don't need to. Crissy already told us the girl can't dance. We know she doesn't have a drug habit, as well. Beyond that, however, she is a ghost. No one gets that deep underground yet works for a man like Mud. This is someone we need to keep our eyes on.

Hammer taps away on his phone beside me, while Coal sits with his elbows on the table, resting his chin on his hands as he watches her perform with a blank stare. Knowing my brother, he is seeing straight through her. She is vapor, smoke, nothing more than a movement in time. Skid is leaning back in his chair, arms crossed behind his head, watching her with a cocky smirk.

"Come give me a lap dance. You bring it to life"—he points at his jean covered cock—"you get a job."

She sighs, hesitating.

She is obviously not meant to shake her ass on a stage. Since I don't have any information in her file, I have no idea why she is trying to force herself to do it.

What I do know is that I can't put crap-ass talent in front of my paying customers.

"Done," I bark out at her.

As humiliation washes over her face, I can see the tears well up in her eyes. Not letting one tear fall, she bends over to gather her discarded clothes while the four of us slide our chairs back and stand.

"Be here Friday at six. You don't dance, you waitress. We will handle giving your notice to Mud," I state, watching the words sink in and the relief take over her.

"Get some clothes. Short shorts, no skirts, tank tops, and heels," Coal orders, tossing down money on the table.

Morgan

It has been two months without any issues from my sister. She will graduate high school in a little less than two months. My parents still won't let her come home. I can't believe it, but I am okay with having her here. Actually, I like having her around. It is nice to come home and know it won't be to an empty house.

Walking in, I am expecting quiet since Madyson stayed home from school today due to not feeling well. However, I don't expect to find her bedroom empty. Something doesn't feel right. She left no note, but there is also no sign of anyone else being here. Calming my overactive imagination, I go about my evening.

When it is well past a decent time for a respectable young lady to be home, I call her phone. No answer. Her voicemail sounds with her cheery teen voice, pulling at my heart.

Where are you, Madyson?

After the beep, I quickly reply, "I know it's only ten, but Mom's training has kicked into my brain. Where are you? I just want to know you are safe."

The night passes in a blur of anxiety. What is she doing? Is she okay? Why is she acting out now? Things have been absolutely great lately. What has changed? These thoughts run through my head. My emotions are a rollercoaster I want nothing more than to get off of. One moment I am worried, the next I am angry, and then I find myself sad that maybe my sister is rebelling because even this last bit hasn't been enough to overcome the damage our parents have inflicted. With every change in thought and emotion, I fire off another call or a text to Madyson. Finally, with her voicemail full, I am left with only texting and waiting impatiently for her to reply.

No matter how hard I try to stay awake, I slowly start to feel my eyelids getting heavier and heavier. I get up and walk around my living room, hoping the physical activity will help, although I am so tired my legs feel like they are full of lead. Therefore, I head into my kitchen and make myself a pot of coffee. With each cup I consume, my anxiety increases. I would give anything, right now, simply to get a text message from Madyson, letting me know she is okay. Instead, my phone stays eerily silent. I pass out on the couch with my fourth cup of coffee still in my hand, and my last thought before oblivion is hoping my phone rings so my little sister can tell me she is okay.

The annoying beep on my cell phone's alarm clock makes me jump up from the couch. Looking around, momentarily confused as to why I was sleeping on the couch, I see my spilled cup of coffee on the cushions, and it all rushes back to me. Madyson. Waiting for her to come home last night, hoping to get a call or a text from her.

Looking down at my phone, I see my hopes were for nothing. The screen is blank. The house is still silent, but I won't let that dash my fleeting optimism that maybe she snuck in after I passed out and is sleeping in her room.

I race to her room and don't bother to knock before I throw open the door while holding my breath. It escapes in a ragged exhale of unease when I see her empty bed. Not willing to give up hope just yet, I run throughout my place, calling her name, praying she is somewhere, anywhere in here. I would even be willing not to scream and yell at her for scaring me if she would only be safely inside our home.

My prayers go unanswered, though.

Maybe I should call the police? But then it occurs to me that Madyson is eighteen now. They won't look for her under the guise that she is a runaway. Nor do I have any suspicious evidence that I can point to for foul play. All I have is an empty house and a missing teenager who is known to get into trouble.

The only place I can think she might be is with Brooke. Giving Madyson the benefit of the doubt that maybe her phone broke or she wasn't thinking because Mom and Dad would never chase her down, I send a text to Brooke to check in. When the reply comes back that Madyson is not with her, my heart sinks. Asking her to have Madyson call me when she gets to school is my only hope to reach my sister today.

Having no choice, I get ready for the day and head off to work. The day is full of distraction to the point that I have to stop meeting clients.

Brooke sends me a text on her lunch break to say Madyson did not come to school. My instincts are screaming at me that something is wrong. After a text from Mallory that she hasn't heard from Madyson, either, I am really on edge. She may be reckless, but this is far from her typical behavior.

Breaking down, I call the people I have never asked for help. I have spent my entire life fitting into the box they have created for me. Not once have I questioned anything or asked anything additional from them.

"Morgan, hello, dear." My mother's voice sends a chill down my spine.

I love my parents in the obligatory way, as in they gave me life; however, I am far from happy with them. Most girls are close with either their mother or their father, but I am not. There is a deeply rooted insecurity within me that I will fail them at every turn. I have no idea why I am so concerned with pleasing them, though. Honestly, I don't know if therapy could even undo the brainwashing I have endured.

My life with my family has always been to stay within the boundaries and do not fail, until Madyson started rebelling that is. Mallory followed suit, and I watched jealously as my sisters found themselves while I continued to plaster on the fake smile and be the Morgan they all expected. If I am real with myself, until Madyson got into trouble and needed to live with me, my entire existence has been about my parents' desires for a perfect child.

"Mom, have you heard from Madyson?" I ask, knowing I am possibly digging a hole for my sister, myself, or even both of us.

"I don't know who that is or why she would call us." My mother's cold reply further infuriates me.

"Don't be like this, please."

"Whatever do you mean?"

"Mom, I can't find Madyson."

"And this is my problem, why exactly?" she questions coldly. "Your cousin mailed us a thank you for attending her wedding and for our gift. She was wondering if you will ever get married since you didn't bring a date. A date we requested you find and you didn't. Now we have questions to answer."

The audacity of her quickly and easily changing the subject adds to my anger. No longer able to contain myself, I explode. "It doesn't matter when or *if* I get married. That wedding was show and tell for the family. She's already sleeping with the best man. Seriously, get a clue. I'm so over you and everything you stand for."

"What does that mean? We are a family. You are my daughter, my only daughter."

"You are sick and twisted. Go get some help. You have three beautiful, amazing, intelligent daughters, but your head is too far up your own butt to see it. I have nothing left to say to you. *And*, if you are going to feel that way about Mallory, pack her up and send her to me. There is no reason for them to continue to feel less than perfect because you have some warped ideal family when you have awesomely unique children who are perfect in their own rights."

Ending the call, I wipe away the tears that are freely falling. Now, more than ever, I need to find Madyson.

Chapter

8

Ice

"Count is up to three this month. It's increasing," Hammer states to the room of Regulators.

Looking around the room, I take in the posters of naked pin-up models draped over Harleys. Then I move my attention to the large, hand-painted, wooden sign on one wall that bears our insignia of an eagle holding the sword of justice with 'Regulators' over the top of it. I feel that familiar sense of purpose wash over me.

This room is a far cry from the sort of 'War Rooms' we have been in the past—the numerous sterile rooms with their white walls and uniformity —but this is our 'War Room.' It is the place where we hold 'sermon,' otherwise known as the meetings where we decide whose ass needs kicking or what we are doing as a club next. Now my men are waiting for information on one of the biggest problems we have looked into since we hit the Miami area.

We sit around a large, rectangular, sturdy, wooden table with four chairs down each side and two chairs on each end. I sit at one end while Coal as the VP sits to my side. If Coal is considered my 'right hand,' then Hammer, as my Sergeant of Arms, is my 'left.' Big Jim, the large redheaded bastard who joined my Army Special Forces team when we were in the desert, sits at the opposite end of the table as my Road Captain. The rest of the men fill the chairs in between.

All of my men are ex-military, all of them green berets that have served with me, Coal, or Hammer at some time. No one who saw us now would be able to discern that. Some of these boys have taken to the role of becoming a mean-ass biker like a duck takes to water. Of course, we have been living this life for years. We have not only come to accept it, but we enjoy it. We are more than former military men now.

We are the Regulators MC, a group of men not to be fucked with. A band of brothers who have walked through blood, bullets, and war to come home and dish out our own kind of blood, bullets, and war. Only, this time, we don't have some pansy ass commanding officer giving us orders. The boys have me, and as I stare at them sitting around the table, I know the respect they give me has been earned doing shit overseas that is far worse than what we do now.

We might put blood on our hands in different ways these days, but the perks that offset the life we live make it worth it. Freedom to run our shit the way we want to run it: pussy, booze, and no tight-assed dickwads issuing orders to us. Life is good.

Until this shit landed on our doorstep.

We watch as women keep disappearing randomly and regularly for over a year now. At first, the missing women didn't stay on our radar because the victims were randomly spaced out. There was nothing to indicate that it was the same person behind all of the kidnappings.

Then I came across some classified information, via Screech, that had the hair on the back of my neck standing on end.

Another Army brother of mine and Hammer's, Lucas Young, was working a case with his nifty little black ops crew, the Ex Ops Team. They moonlighted as a private security force, but I had intel that indicated they were a hell of a lot more than that. As in, the men the government sent in to solve their worst problems without the public ever finding out. Not that I could tell Lucas I knew about his gig. No one other than the head of Homeland Security and the President are supposed to know about them.

When Screech told me they were looking for the person or persons behind the kidnapping of one 'Laura Moore,' a petite yet curvy, redheaded stripper who had gone missing from our area almost a year ago, I knew the problem was a lot worse than we originally thought.

When I got a call from Lucas asking some questions that raised my suspicions of their activities, I decided to take a chance. I slipped him the information about the missing women to lure his team down here. It might seem shitty to lure an old friend into a dangerous situation, but I knew Lucas could take care of himself. A team like theirs wouldn't be filled with pansy ass-wipes who couldn't complete a mission, so I had no qualms using them to my ends.

Having their team come down wasn't because I needed them to solve our problem. No, it had more to do with the feeling I had that, if the Ex Ops Team came down here, it might help our own investigation. With what they were working on, I felt it was a mutually beneficial exchange of resources.

I offered them an undercover guise as men in my crew. Gave them cuts, bikes to borrow, and the information I had acquired on the string of missing women Screech had uncovered all across the south. In return, their presence and operation provided me a name to head in the right direction.

Lazaro Sandoval, head of the expanding Cuban Mafia.

We can't say a hundred percent that he is the person behind the kidnappings, but it is a place to start looking.

However, if I'd known having Lucas and his team coming here would cost me Kara, I probably wouldn't have slipped them the tip they needed. Call me an asshole, but a man knows when he has a good woman around. Too bad I wasn't the man meant to keep her.

Our area has the usual homeless population; as a result, the slow rise of middle class women going missing is alarming. Add to it the most recent climb in numbers, and the hair on my neck is standing up. The targets aren't housewives or upscale citizens, but they are working women—strippers, to be exact. The hookers and street whores selling pussy for dope are accounted for, for the most part. In narrowing down the subjects, it seems to be focused on young, female strippers.

"Latest one isn't even legal or stripping," Coal adds, shaking his head in disgust. "She got her job with a fake ID, according to her friend. She's only seventeen. Dad was molesting her. Mom didn't believe her. She ran away, got a job waitressing at Paisty's. Now, she's been gone nine days. Her roommate says she hasn't been back at all. Nothing missing, nothing touched, and her purse with her real ID is still at home."

"We have any leads on how she was nabbed?" I ask. If we did, the boys would have piped up with the information, but I am desperate for something.

"Nothing. She's a ghost, just like the others."

"We have spent months trying to find the pattern to the disappearances. Obviously, we aren't going to be able to prevent the next one from turning up missing. We need to get a lead on where the girls are being held," Rocks pipes in.

"Well, maybe you aren't dumb as rocks after all. Who's to say they are being held, though? Realistically, these girls could have been raped, killed, and the bodies dumped in the damn ocean. All we have is one instance of one of the girls, Laura Moore, being found in the hands of the Rivera Cartel by the Ex Ops Team. All the other girls are dead ends. Laura's not exactly breathing these days, boys; we can't count on the fact that the other girls are breathing, either," Hammer says, bringing up the worst case scenario.

"No, word would get out on the street. Plus, if it was happening like that, it would be a one man show. By this point, he would have slipped up and made a mistake. Whatever this is, it's big, and it has to involve some key players and multiple people. They are targeting women the cops wouldn't waste their time on, women who don't have family or friends with resources to do big search parties. This is meticulous and well thought through as to not draw attention from the boys in blue or the locals." I look at Coal so he can see where my thoughts are going.

"That description certainly fits Sandoval." He nods.

"Exactly what I was thinking. This is why we're going to stay on Sandoval's trail. We may not have all the proof we need, but at the moment, he's still our best bet. Let's call a meet. He's in bed pretty deep with us now on the drugs and guns. Let's see if he will sell us some pussy. You have the way in for us there, Coal. Make your call, get me in."

Coal has a dark past. He doesn't have sex he doesn't pay for, and for once, that is going to pay off for us all, I hope. Sandoval has a pimp pushing his girls on the streets. When Coal doesn't want it from our girls, he has used theirs. Sandoval doesn't know that we are aware it is his stable, but he will soon find out.

If I can get Sandoval to sell me some of his girls to come work for me, maybe I can link them to at least one of these missing women. One break is all we need. We only need to find one of these women alive and go backwards to sort out how they were taken.

With a new angle to follow, we break the meeting so the guys can get back to their jobs, and I can sort my own shit to be ready for Sandoval's next available time to negotiate. If I am able to work a deal for some girls, we need to be prepared.

"Coal, get Crissy to ready some space. Just in case we can get a girl, we need to have a place for her."

Lining up our plans is one thing; the hard part of waiting is another. Will Sandoval open this avenue of his business to us? Everything has to be a calculated risk. Normally, I wouldn't push further into his world this soon, but the disappearances are coming far too frequently to sit back and wait.

My stomach tightens. This whole business disgusts me. It is one thing for us to save women from their own addictions and shadows of their pasts. They willingly sell their bodies. Whoever is taking these women and doing who knows what with them, is taking away their choices.

Hopefully, pushing for more doesn't arouse any suspicion from Sandoval. The whole mess feels as if we are getting further in bed with the devil.

Morgan

It has been three long days and three even longer nights, without any word or sign of my sister. I have cried, I have paced, and I have prayed for any clue as to where she is. Brooke hasn't heard from her either, only heightening my concerns. I am borderline hysterical when I leave to go see Casey. I don't know what she can do precisely, but maybe she can give me some direction to follow in the seedier parts of town.

Arriving at the club, I didn't give a second thought to Casey's job. After a quick text, she greets me outside. A silk robe covers her body, and she is wearing sky high stilettos that I am sure I would fall and break my neck if I wore.

"Still nothing?" she asks as I climb out of my car.

The dam on my emotions burst, and I can't hold back the barrage of tears any longer. As my body shakes in sobs, Casey takes my hand and guides me inside the back entrance and to the dressing room. She hugs me close until I am able to settle enough to pull away and look at her.

"I called the police. They said because she is eighteen they won't help me, which I sort of knew would happen, but I hoped they would help anyways, since she just turned eighteen not that long ago. Why won't they help me, Casey?"

"They're assuming she's a runaway, and you know what they say about assuming. The cops around here are nothing but asses, honey. Since she doesn't live at home with your parents and she is of legal age, what more can they do?"

There is a change in music and Casey's eyes grow big. I stare at her in confusion, although before I can ask her what is wrong, the dressing room door opens.

"Why the fuck do I have music playing and no headliner?" the biggest jerk of my world barks out angrily.

Why is he everywhere I don't want him to be?

"I... I... I..." Casey stutters.

Gathering my courage, I clear my throat, pushing down the lump that has formed. "It's my fault. I was having a problem, and Casey is my friend. I'm sorry, I shouldn't have come here." I start to get up to leave.

"Damn right you shouldn't be here. I sell beautiful women, and tonight, you are far from beautiful." He takes in my appearance of yoga pants and a T-shirt. My hair is in a messy knot on top of my head, and I am certain my eyes are swollen and face splotchy from all the crying.

"Don't go anywhere, Morgan. I'll be four minutes and thirty-eight seconds." Casey looks at me, pleading for me to hang tight.

"The hell she will. I'm sorry some fucker in a suit broke your heart, but you two can whine over some ice cream another night. Casey, you have a job to do, and she is a distraction, one that's costing me money. Get your ass to work." Glaring at me, Ice adds, "You, get your ass out of here unless you plan to doll up and work a pole."

"My sister is missing. She's been gone three days," I explain. I don't know why I am sharing this with him, but it ticks me off that he assumed I would bother Casey at work over boy problems.

"She'll turn up," he states before turning back to Casey. "Ass. Pole. Now," he clips before exiting the room.

"Stay put, Morgan. Let me get through this dance, and we'll talk to Hammer."

"Fuck no," I firmly state, causing Casey's eyes to go wide at my language. "I want nothing from *that* man or his friends. He has been rude to me more times than I care to count. I don't know him, and I haven't done anything to him. Plus, there is no way in hell he will help me find Madyson. He can't even stand to be in the same room with me."

"Things aren't always what they seem, Morgan. He's not all bad. Hammer is easier to talk to. I promise, he will listen."

Before I can respond, we hear Ice bellow her name from down the hall.

Casey takes off out of the room. Looking over her shoulder one last time, she calls out to me, "Stay put."

Should I stay? Probably. Idle waiting is not getting me anywhere, though. Needing to feel like I am doing something for my sister, I leave Casey a note promising to call tomorrow. Tonight, I need to hit the streets and find my sister.

Chapter

9

Ice

"Could he be expanding his victim profile?" I ask Hammer and Coal as we sit in my office, trying to sort out what may have happened to Madyson Powell.

Coal shrugs. "Not sure. Could be."

"Brooke is freaked the hell out. She swears there is no way Madyson would just disappear like this. According to Brooke, Madyson may have hated her parents, but she loves her sister. She wouldn't do this to her," I murmur while rubbing a finger absentmindedly over my bottom lip.

Hammer laughs sarcastically at me. "Well, asshole, if you had been a little more hospitable, the chick might have considered sticking around last night rather than taking off."

"I thought she was being dramatic about a break up, not that her sister was gone. Bottom line, Casey missed her cue, and we were packed. Morgan brought her shit to our doorstep and cost us money."

Coal shakes his head at me. "This is not about the money. You know Casey missing one cue doesn't make or break the bank for you, the business, or the club. Cut the shit, Ice. This girl shakes you up."

If I am honest with myself, yes, she does. There is an innocence to Morgan Powell that isn't found in anyone else. She has a genuine sweetness that comes off her in waves. Reaching down, I adjust my cock to remind me that I have one. In my line of work and in my life, I can't afford to be soft for anyone or anything.

"Call Casey in here. Let's see what we can do to sort this out."

"Yup, Miss Prim and Proper has you shaken up," Hammer laughs.

"Not the time, fucker. I'm not shaken. I have a business to run. Between her sister and her, I can't run my business, that's all."

"You need to get laid, asshole. Let off some steam, work out some aggression." Hammer's still smiling at me as he walks out the door to get Casey.

What my Sergeant of Arms does not know is that I have already tried to blow off some damn steam to try and unwind. Hell, I know I am wound tight. But the very reason I am wound so tight is also the reason why I walked out on the barfly who was on her knees ready to suck my dick. Because I looked down at the barfly's face, over done with eye makeup so dark she looked like a fucking raccoon, and all I could think was that I would rather be looking down at Morgan's naturally pretty face instead. The woman is starting to get under my skin and I have no idea how she got there. I don't have time for this shit.

"If Madyson Powell was taken under the same circumstances as the other missing strippers, then this whole thing has become personal," Coal states, bringing us back to the severity of the situation. "It's one thing for us to be looking for missing strippers around the area, but to be looking for one of Brooke's friends, that's too close to home for my liking."

A knock on the door draws all of our attention.

"Enter," I call out.

Only a moment later, the door opens and Casey enters. "Am I getting fired? I'm sorry I missed my cue. Morgan needed me. I couldn't just take off. It won't happen again." Her job obviously means something to her for her to get this worked up over one infraction.

"Breathe. You aren't getting fired," I state, trying to calm her down. "Today."

Before I can start to explain the reason for calling her in, she is spouting off excuses at us again.

"If you're writing me up, I understand. Please hear me out, though. Morgan, she's not one to get upset easily like that. Her sister is wild, but not stupid. She wouldn't just disappear. And, see, Morgan has some really strange parents. Her home life, it's not what you or I would call normal-."

I throw my hand up to stop her. "You're not one to bring up someone else's home life." I know her history. Her upbringing was far from normal. "I don't need the autobiography of Morgan Ann Powell. I do, however, need to know what happened to her sister or, at least, what she thinks happened."

"Honestly, I haven't been able to get her to answer her damn phone since you ran her off. When I went by her apartment, she wasn't there. Morgan isn't close to many people. She doesn't have anyone to turn to for this. I don't know where she is now or what she's doing."

Everything inside me goes tight. What does Casey mean she can't find her? I may not like the woman, but I certainly don't want her caught up in this shit.

Tipping my head back to look at the ceiling, I wonder if anyone upstairs can answer just one question for me.

Why the fuck are women so damn frustrating?

Morgan

"Miss Powell, as we have stated previously, your sister is eighteen. It doesn't matter that she is still in high school; she is a legal adult. We will file your missing persons report; however, understand that our priorities will be to find her, not to bring her home."

I glance around the rundown police station in frustration, looking for somebody, anybody, that looks like they might be more compassionate and capable than this jerk. Unfortunately, I don't see anyone who looks like they care in this place.

Several officers crowd around one desk in the back corner, laughing at something one of them has said. Another officer is sitting at his desk, playing a game on his computer. None of them are paying a lick of attention to the woman sitting in one of the plastic chairs against the wall crying. Casey was so right when she said these guys are asses.

Looking back to the balding officer whose pot belly strains the buttons of his stained uniform, I feel some of my patience snap. "Priority," I huff the word in exasperation. "You sit here, Officer Dillard, and tell me you won't bring her home because it's not a priority. What I'm trying to explain to you is that this should be a freakin' priority! I know my sister, and she wouldn't leave like this."

"We took your report; now move along so we can do our job," he answers me emotionlessly.

Move along. I can't believe this patronizing peon really just told me to move along! I can't believe no one will help me. The fact that the man can sit there, as if he does not care one bit over a missing eighteen-year-old girl while his hand keeps inching over to that jelly donut he put down when I walked in, pisses me off.

At my wits end, I slap my hand down on the surface of his desk as I stand up to leave. Then, pointing a finger at his face, I snap, "Here's your new priority for the day, Officer Dillard, stop stuffing your face with stuff you obviously don't need to be eating and get up off your ass and do a better job of showing the citizens of your jurisdiction that you actually give a shit."

I leave the police station, and a feeling of defeat overtakes me. I am not equipped to search for her. I don't even know where to begin. Calling the hospitals has come up empty each and every day. The more time that ticks by, the more helpless I feel.

The sympathetic secretary at the police station did suggest I check the homeless shelters. With no other options presenting themselves, I make my way to the first one on the list that she gave me.

Parking my car, I stare at the medium-sized building, thinking it can't possibly be big enough to hold that many people. As I walk inside, though, I see the people who run this place have done the best they can with their resources.

The room in front of me is large, open, and has a friendly atmosphere, despite the circumstances for why one would need to be here. There are at least a hundred cots spaced out with wool blankets and pillows on every one. Some of those cots are already full with ragged and tattered looking men, women, and children. My heart breaks at seeing some of them so obviously defeated.

Along the back wall is a stainless steel counter, manned by a few volunteers who are dishing out food to those who are waiting in line with trays. There are so many people here, way more than the hundred or so cots that are visible. I can't help wondering what happens to those who don't get a cot. Do they sleep on the floor? Are they kicked out of the building at night?

With each passing thought, my eyes water a little more. It takes everything I have not to break down and cry for what is probably the thousandth time since Madyson went missing.

While staring at the room, one of the volunteers cautiously approaches me. "Miss, do you need some help?"

Looking somewhat blindly at the woman, I hear my voice rasp, "I'm looking for my little sister. Her name is Madyson. She's eighteen years old. Hold on." Digging through my purse, I pull out her picture. "Here, this is what she looks like. Have you seen her? She's been missing for four days, and I'm desperate to find her." I can hear the hope in my voice.

Silently I pray the kind looking woman in front of me has seen my little sister, but when she shakes her head and gives me a sad look, I know my prayers went unheard.

"I'm sorry, sweetie, but I haven't seen her here. Feel free to walk the room and look around, though. I know that would make you feel better. Just please don't get to close to anyone. They don't like it when someone invades their space. It's hard for them living on the streets, and the small things, like personal space and safety, are sometimes the only things they have left to hold on to."

I nod my head dejectedly at the woman before thanking her for her help. After going through the place with no sign of my sister, I move onto the next two facilities with no luck. It is like she vanished. No one has seen her, knows her, or honestly, seems to care.

The drive home is a blur as the tears run freely down my face. Not paying attention to anything around me, I make my way to my doorstep only to stop in my tracks.

Leaning against my door in his jeans, black T-shirt, and leather vest is none other than Ice.

As if I don't have enough going wrong in my life! Let's add something else to the crap-tastic day I am having.

"Brooke's not here, or she shouldn't be," I quickly say, hoping he will leave.

"Oh, I'm very aware of where Brooke is. I can't say the same for your sister, but no worries about my daughter."

Cocky bastard. All of my energy has been spent on the search for my sister; I don't have it in me to fight with him today.

"Why are you here, then? I really don't have time for your brand of asshole."

He smiles, really, genuinely, full blown smiles. Something shifts in the air around me. My anger remains firmly planted at the surface, though I see something deeper into this man before me suddenly.

"My brand of asshole, huh? You're cute, Morgan. I'm here to help."

"Help?" I question out loud unintentionally. Why does he want to help now? He turned me away. Harshly, brutally, without cause, without a second glance, and without care, he turned me away. Now he stands at my doorstep, offering to help? I want nothing more than to refuse him. The independent side of me wants to scream, yell, throw things, and yes, have a full blown temper tantrum that I don't need a single thing from him. The truth is, however, I do. I do need his help, his connections, and even the bad boy edge he carries. He is the only hope I have left for finding my sister.

"Can we go inside?" he asks, looking at the keys still in my hand.

No! I scream inside my head. No, we can't go inside. No, you can't simply be nice now. He owes me an apology at the very least. Is this how all women are around him? He acts like the biggest dick on the planet until he decides to give me a chance and what now? Am I supposed to bow down and thank him?

My entire life has been doing what everyone wants and expects from me. He is no different. I am tired of being walked all over and treated like crap. No more.

"Why? I have nothing to say to you. Madyson is my problem, not yours."

He shakes his head at me and blows out a breath. "You're gonna make me say it, aren't you?"

Confusion covers my features. "Huh?"

"Fine. I was wrong. I'm here to make it right and help find Madyson."

Surprise hits me at his admission. His attitude must be rubbing off on me because I can't stop myself from challenging him further. "Wrong about what exactly? Wrong about my irresponsibility? Wrong about my sister? Wrong about my intentions with your daughter? Wrong about why I was at your business to see my friend? Which, I will add, I had no idea you were her boss, or I would've steered clear. So, yes, Ice, please tell me which infraction you are owning up to because there are many."

"I was wrong about you. All of it. Everything. I'm an ass of epic proportions," he states easily.

"And…" I know I am playing with fire. I see it dance in his eyes.

Suddenly, he is in my personal space, and I am backing up against the wall. His hands come up to on either side of my face. "What are you looking for exactly, Morgan? Let's stop the bullshit and cut to the chase."

My chest rises and falls in rapid succession at his close proximity. "An apology. Some respect. I need to find my sister, but I don't need to feel like crap doing it. I won't beg you." I drop my eyes, unable to handle the intensity of his stare.

"You're cute, Morgan. Understand this, I make no apologies. Ever. I am who I am. I'm all man. I'm also man enough to admit when I'm wrong. I did that. Sorry-- I'm not sorry. Everything I do, right or wrong, serves a purpose." He tips my chin up, forcing me to look at him again. "My word is solid, and I give you my word I will find your sister somehow, someway. Morgan, you get me—my help—but, sweetheart, what you don't get is my apology. We clear?"

At my nod, he pushes off the wall, giving us both space. Shaking my head to clear my thoughts, I make my way over to open the door. Once inside, I watch as Ice takes in my space. Inside, I feel slightly invaded having him unexpectedly in my personal area.

"What do you know?" he questions, bringing me out of my insecurities.

"Nothing really. She stayed home from school because she was having cramps." His eyes blink in what I could assume to be a cringe at my honesty before he quickly hides behind the mask of meanness once again. "Old lady Hanover said she saw her leave around ten a.m. Madyson apparently greeted her and offered to pick her up some milk from the drug store on the corner. She was going to get some pain meds and chocolate. That was the last anyone has seen or heard from her."

"That's a starting point. Does she have any enemies at school? A boyfriend?"

I shake my head at his questions. "Believe it or not, other than my parents' issues with her, my sister is well liked."

"What do you know of your parents' financial situation?"

"They're fine. What do they have to do with this?" The hair on the back of my neck stands up. The look in Ice's eyes shows he knows more than he is letting on. It is not my place to divulge my parent's financial situation to anyone. I can't help but wonder if he already knows. They aren't rolling in money. They have quite a bit of debt, but they are getting by.

"Do you trust me?" He locks his gaze with mine so he can gage my answer.

"No," I answer with complete honesty. This he returns with that breathtaking smile of his.

"Cute and smart. I could possibly like you after all, Morgan Powell."

"I don't need you to like me. I need to find my sister, you can help or you can move on."

"What if I told you your parents are in some serious debt?"

"I would say my dad has a good job, but my mom likes to spend. They're fine, though. What does that have to do with my sister?"

"Your parents aren't fine. They're on the verge of losing everything." His words rock me. I stumble to get to my couch to sit down.

"What are you saying, Ice?" I knew they overspent and had some debt, but is it that bad?

"I'm not saying anything for sure. What I'm doing is gathering information so I can sort out the facts and follow the leads to get your sister. This means I have to keep an open mind. Desperate people do desperate things."

"They wouldn't," I whisper, not really knowing if I am right or not.

Would they do something crazy to Madyson to pay off a debt? Are they worse off than I know? I have even more questions than answers now and more concerns than ever before.

Chapter
10

Ice

"Where are we now?"

The room is packed. Every patched member of the Regulators MC is present. Every man in this room is deadly and has some sort of special skill set: sniper, explosives, hand to hand combat. We are not exactly a group of men you want to fuck with.

"From what we gathered on nearby cameras, Madyson Powell was walking to the drug store. She was approached at the right side of the building. The guy was in dark and torn clothing. For an unknown reason, she followed him to the back corner where there is no angle on a camera. Beyond that moment, there is no further visual of her anywhere," Rocks informs the group.

"Where are we with the next Sandoval meet?" I ask, needing confirmation. Sandoval won't meet with just anyone. It has to be me each and every time, which means I adjust to his availability.

"Tonight. We are due dock side at midnight," Coal answers promptly, checking his watch as if to calculate our count down.

"Map out the points. Set up teams. As soon as he pulls out, I want every single one of them followed.

Screech, hack into every system you can: GPS on their cars, phones. I don't care what it takes, track everything. If we can find where the girls are, we have hope."

The men all nod at me. "Screech, have you found anything more on the Powell's financial situation?"

"Has this become personal?" Hammer watches me intently for my answer.

"No, I'm covering all our bases, making sure there isn't a loan shark involved who's looking for leverage in a teen girl," I bark back at him.

"You seem on edge, brother. Is this gonna be a problem?" Hammer asks in his same casual tone, always the calm one. He has never been one to question me. I don't know why the fuck he feels the need to start now.

I am out of my seat and in his face before anyone can move. "Have I ever led you wrong? Are you gonna fuckin' question me now? Innocent women are disappearing left and right. Commander Wall and his team gathered the initial intel that brought us to Sandoval. We have been investigating and building up to this. Why question me now?"

"Not questioning the task at hand, only gauging where your head is. You're pushing hard and fast. We need to know if this is personal."

"Fuck no, why would it be?" I snarl back at him.

"A certain big sister comes to mind." Coal wears a sinister smirk.

"Where the hell do you assholes get off?" My anger rises.

"Last night, I got off with Crissy," Coal eggs me on.

"Fuck you!"

"Cute chick, and yup, she has you shaken. No worries, Prez, we got your back. We'll get your woman's sister back," Hammer taunts.

"She's not my woman!" I explode. "Madyson is Brooke's friend. People care about her. This doesn't fit the other missing girls. We could end up in two different directions here. We cannot afford to miss any details."

"We get that, brother, but you've never been this wound up. Check that shit before we're in too deep," Coal orders, making me stop and think.

Shit. The truth hits me harder than a case of C4. I won't admit it to him, but he is right. What is it about Morgan Powell that winds me up like a coo-coo clock ready to spring?

Morgan

Walking into my parents' home, I am taken aback at the removal of all reminders of Madyson. Not that there were many in the first place; however, what little there was is now gone. For instance, the family picture my mother had hanging in the dining room where my sisters and I pasted on fake smiles and pretended we were the perfect, happy little family that our parents wanted us to be. That picture is now missing, and in its place, there is an oversized portrait of my mother and father.

There had also been a couple of pictures stationed strategically around our old family portrait. Two pictures each of Madyson, Mallory, and myself. Those pictures are now missing, as well. It is as if they are trying to erase any evidence they could of their children. In its place is now a house that gives the impression that two well-to-do adults live here. How is my youngest sister Mallory taking these changes?

My mother sits on her settee, sipping tea like she has not a care in the world. All while my sister—her daughter—could be in trouble or worse.

Tears pool up in my eyes at the thought of what Madyson could be enduring.

"Mom, why did you take her pictures down?"

"Whose, dear?" she asks, pretending to be baffled.

"Seriously? Madyson. Your middle daughter."

My mother takes another slow sip of her tea before nonchalantly answering, "She is gone. She didn't want to be a part of our family. Rather than have to explain ourselves, we took her away."

"She wanted to be a family. You kicked her out."

"Actions speak louder than words, Morgan. She didn't act accordingly. Mallory has learned from her mistakes."

My blood runs cold. What does she mean Mallory has learned from Madyson's mistakes? Is Mallory in danger of being kicked out, too?

My mind races with worry at the thought that my other little sister is now living in fear of being kicked out of the only home she has ever known. How could my parents be this callous?

"Your daughter is missing!" I shout. "How can you sit here drinking tea like nothing is wrong?"

"She is eighteen. She is free to be. Nothing is wrong."

Bile rises up in my throat at her words. How easily she tosses us aside for not fitting her mold. What kind of sick, twisted spin has she given herself in her head to justify this?

Looking around one last time, I realize this is a lost cause. I don't know how or when yet, but I need to speak to Mallory then possibly find a lawyer. There is no way I can leave my other sister to suffer this nightmare anymore. My parents have gone from delusional and self-involved to deranged. First, however, I have to find Madyson.

Without another word, I turn and leave. Like a robot, I walk to my car, get in, and drive without truly thinking about what I am doing or where I am going. Instinctively, I end up at After Midnight. I don't know why I came here, only that I can't go home and find my place empty yet again. Any time I try to do it, the pain I feel from the silence of my house manifests so profoundly I feel like I am being stabbed in the heart. My chest seizes up, and I end up crying till I pass out because I am still not sleeping at night due to the fear for Madyson.

Spotting Casey's car in the back lot, I find relief in being able to see her. Timorously, I make my way to the club entrance.

The burly man at the door does nothing to ease my mood. He towers over me with his beard and huge frame. The black leather vest he wears has a patch that says Hulk on it. Hulk he is, that's for sure.

"Whatcha need, darlin'? You applyin' for a job?" he greets me with a grin.

"I... I... I'm here to see Casey," I stammer stupidly.

"Can't let ya in that easy."

Oh, my God! He wouldn't dare expect sexual favors from me to get in, right? Last time I came in the back door. I should have done that this time, too. I was such a mess the guy at the back door didn't even question me especially with Casey with me. I should have just called her to come escort me inside.

My fear must show when the man lets out a hearty laugh letting me know he was joking with me. "Go on in. Don't know if she'll have clothes on or not. If that's your thing, it's hot. Have a good time, sugar tits."

Rather than bark back at him and his last remark, I walk through the door he holds open for me.

When I walk through to the back, the sight before me makes me halt in my tracks. What is the phrase? What has been seen cannot be unseen? That is exactly how I feel right now. Everywhere I look, women are in some stage of undress. Some are taking off their clothes, while others are taking off their stage costumes to put their clothes on. All of them make me feel insecure about my own body. Not to mention, the state of the room sends my OCD into high gear.

There is stuff everywhere. Clothes on the floor and vanity chairs. Bags and purses on the floors against the walls instead of hanging on the hooks or lockers provided to them. I watch as one woman throws a stiletto at another woman, which causes a catfight. It is pure pandemonium. How the heck does my best friend work in this every day? It would drive me nuts to be back here, even if I did have the guts to strip naked on a stage in front of strange men.

I scan the women, bending my head this way and that to look around those who are standing up in front of others and those who are sitting at the vanities, putting on their make-up.

I am still searching for Casey in the dressing rooms when I hear his voice. I shiver and my veins run cold. Is that why they call him Ice? Does he have this effect on everyone? Even with our newfound truce, I am far from comfortable with him.

I am barely keeping myself together when Ice is suddenly standing in front of me.

"Morgan, are you okay?" The tone in his voice is laced with compassion, care, understanding, and kindness. There is not one trace of the broody, anger-enriched, aggravated tones of the past.

Using my hands, I cover my face to hide the tears that are threatening to fall as I stand there silently. When his two strong arms embrace me, pulling me into his solid chest, I lose it completely. All the emotions I have tried and failed to contain spill out on his black leather vest. His hands softly rub my back in an attempt to soothe while I continue to sob helplessly in his arms.

Who knew the one person I would never want to comfort me is also the very person who brings me a little peace through all of my pain?

Chapter
11

Ice

Sometimes, the world in which I live in blackens my soul. The lines get blurred between good and bad. It is survival of the fittest, smartest, and bravest. Daily, I am tested. The world in which I exist is one that requires intelligence, experience, associations, and balls of fucking steel.

The meeting with Sandoval was successful in furthering our connection to him. Lazaro Sandoval, the sick fuck, required one of us to fuck two of the women in front of him after paying for them. Thankfully, Coal only takes pussy he pays for, and initially, didn't mind taking one for the team by trying out the merchandise, so to speak. I can tell his willingness waned when he realized just how out of it the women were. It was obvious in their sloppy interactions and slurred come ons to us that they were high as a kite on something.

For Coal, fucking them, paid for or not, became difficult. He doesn't want to be left with any doubt of their consent. Needless to say, when he finished, he disappeared on us for a while. If we were not in the middle of a job, I would be worried he is somewhere drinking himself to death in order to deal with his demons; however, my VP is a soldier in every way.

Therefore, I know he will not drown himself with alcohol just in case he is needed for the job on short notice. Other than that, I don't have a clue as to where he is. I won't look for him, either. A man should be able to find peace when he needs to.

These aren't high class hookers we are dealing with. According to Coal, the women are definitely drugged to the point of dependency. Their captors more than likely deny them whatever it is they have hooked them on until they are begging for their next hit and forced to sell themselves in order to get it. We have them at the clubhouse detoxing. It is an ugly situation that seems to get darker and deeper by the minute.

"Ice," I answer as my phone rings.

"Got something you need to see, now," Screech says with panic in his voice.

"Be there in ten," I bark back into the phone before disconnecting.

Sending a quick message out to Hammer, Coal, and Skid, I take off to meet everyone at the clubhouse.

Screech has a room here dedicated to his IT equipment. The room is on the small side and extremely cool. He says keeping the temperature down is the best way to ensure his equipment doesn't get overheated. The lights in the room are quite a bit dimmer than my main office. Screech said something about it being better for his eyesight since he sits in front of computer monitors all day. I don't do technology, so if that is what the man needs to do what I need him to do, whatever.

What I do know is that the mysterious atmosphere of low lighting combined with wall to wall gadgets and equipment makes me think of Alfred and Batman down in the bat cave. If I ever told Screech that, the nerdy little bastard would probably bust a nut in comic book glee and buy himself a batman costume. Hence, why I haven't told him that I secretly call this the bat cave.

"Sit down, fellas. You have to watch this," Screech instructs.

"What are we watching exactly?" I ask.

"After the meeting, you had me track everyone. It took me a little longer than usual, but I was able to hack into the feeds coming and going from one Leodanis Gutierrez. He is Sandoval's right hand man and has more access than the rest of Sandoval's crew. I still haven't broken through on Sandoval's phone, but I got enough from Gutierrez to lock in on a live feed. They have the location scrambled; I'm still trying to get an exact location on where the video is being made. At first, I thought it was on a delay, but upon further study, it is indeed a live feed. What you are about to see is unlike anything we have dealt with before."

"Cut the shit and turn it on," Coal clips out. This whole situation has him going back down a dark path.

At the press of a button, the screen comes to life. The grainy images aren't easily discerned, but what we can see is bad enough I grab the arms of my chair in pure rage.

Cages.

Upon cages.

Dog kennels basically line the large room, each one housing a different girl. They are spaced far enough apart that each girl cannot pass items between themselves. Each young woman is chained, as if in prison, hands and ankles together. They are connected to a chain that attaches to a collar that firmly holds a hood over their heads. There is a hole cut out for their mouth, leaving them enough room to eat, spit, or puke; yet, otherwise, rendering the women unable to see what is going on around them.

Some of them must have given trouble of some sort as they have a ball gag strapped across their mouths, and their hands have been moved behind their backs. The lethargy is evident in the body language of each of these girls, making me wonder if they are not being fed, if they have given up, or worse, if they are drugged like the two women we bought from Sandoval. The evidence of their bodily functions is visible on the blankets laid over the cement flooring inside the cages. They are naked, collared, chained, gagged, and helpless to escape the disgust in which they are trapped.

My questions are soon answered when one girls begins to shift in her cage. Her lips move as if she is calling out. Having no audio, we can't tell what she is saying, making each of us feel more helpless.

A large man in a suit comes over to her cage. We watch as he pulls out a vile and needle and injects the girl with an unknown substance.

"Fuck!" I roar out my frustration as the girl immediately succumbs to the drug overtaking her system.

"Using the tattoos of some of the girls, I have been able to identify two of them. The camera is stationary, so my visibility inside the facility is currently limited." Screech points to a blinking light in the corner of the computer monitor. "There are more cameras in the room. I have to hack into their feeds, and then we may be able to match up more girls. This shit takes time, but I'll get in."

"We don't have fuckin' time. They don't have time. We need to know where they are as of yesterday!" Hammer states the obvious.

Staring at the gritty images in front of me, for the first time in my life, I am worried about failing. Because, if I do, these women will be thrust into the depths of an unescapable hell I wouldn't wish upon anyone.

Morgan

The walls are closing in. At least, that is what it feels like as I look around my condo. Feeling overwhelmed at the loss of my sister, the panic creeps up more. Is she ever going to come back? Although I know I can't lose hope, it is hard to hold on with each passing day. At this point, I can't help wondering if she is even still alive.

Needing to do something, anything, to feel productive, I head out to search more. Maybe she stupidly went to the docks. Teenage years are hard. Add the pressure from my parents, maybe she tried drugs and got ahold of something bad.

Looking around, a shiver of unease goes through me. These are not the nice or newer docks of Bayfront Park. No, these are the old, abandoned ones that are no longer being used to receive ships or merchandise. Everything about this area is rundown… and scary.

I have to be careful about where I step because the old, gray, crumbling bricks beneath my feet could cause me to trip and fall. Graffiti covers the abandoned buildings. Every window in these dark and forbidding buildings are either so dirty you can't see through them or broken. The jagged glass feels like a warning of just how dangerous being here is for me.

This area is a known spot for junkies and homeless people. I hope like hell Madyson is not here. Part of me really doesn't think she would come here, simply because she wouldn't want to be surrounded by some place that is so… dirty. However, I have quickly run out of places to search for her, and desperate times call for desperate measures.

Lord knows, by now, I am way beyond being a desperate woman.

I am one step away from being a defeated woman.

"Excuse me," I try to approach a woman with a shopping cart of odds and ends in her collection of life.

"I don't know nothin'," she replies before turning her cart and taking off.

Mentally, I try to keep coaching myself. *I will not be deterred.*

Finding a shirtless man crouched down against a wall with his head against his knees, I think he is a safe place to try again.

"Excuse me," I begin. He doesn't move. "Hello, sir," I try again.

No response.

Tentatively, I reach out and touch his shoulder. He is cool to the touch. No response.

I grip his shoulder and shake slightly, "Mister."

His body slumps over to the side, and it is only then I can see his face. The dried blood coming out of his nose and mouth are one clue to the lifelessness of the body I just touched. His eyes are rolled back into his sunken face. The meth blisters covering his cheeks do nothing to hide the scars from his long term drug use.

My body shakes in anxiety. Faintly, I hear the rumble of what I think to be a loud truck or motorcycle coming. My hands tremble as I stand here, immobile in shock.

"Sexy thing, you're in the wrong part of town," a gravelly voice says from behind me.

When I turn around, the dirtiest man I have ever seen stands before me. Staying stock still, I am at a loss for what to do.

"We're gonna have a good time." He licks his lips at me as if he is ready to devour his last supper.

"I was just leaving." With my flight mode fully kicked in, I make a step to my right to move away, but the man steps in front of me and starts to close in on me. His stench assaults my nose, causing me to shut my eyes and step back, the exact opportunity he needs to reach out and grab my arm.

While panic sets in and I scream, a blur of black comes out of nowhere. The dirty man drops my arm as he is quickly brought to his knees. An elbow to the head knocks him out as my brain catches up slowly to who is saving me.

Ice.

His gorgeous brown eyes cut through me. There is a vulnerability I have never seen before in them.

"What the fuck are you doin'?" he questions in his typical asshole tone.

"Looking for my sister," I croak out.

"Are you trying to get raped or killed?"

"Way to put it nicely. You don't hold any punches, do you?"

"Never," he states calmly as he reaches out a hand. "Come on."

My hand trembles inside his, and he tugs me against him before releasing my hand to hold me against him. Wrapping my arms around him, I draw from his strength, finding comfort in his embrace.

"How did you find me? Why are you here?" I question snuggling into him feeling saved.

"I had a tracker put on your phone after your sister turned up missing. Got a call you were in a bad part of town, a part of town a girl like you should not be in, ever."

Not knowing what to say to his sincere concern for me, I bring us back to what is going on around us. "Ice, I think the man against the wall is dead."

"Yeah, sweetheart, I'm sure he is. We need to get you out of here."

"Shouldn't we call the cops?"

"Because they've been so helpful in looking for Madyson?" My addled brain registers that the sarcasm is not needed, but I don't bother to point it out. I look up into his face to see him staring at me intently. "Let me handle this."

"Okay," I agree and start to pull away, still shaking slightly. Ice stops my retreat and pulls me into his arms, giving me a gentle squeeze. I am surprised by his actions. He might have comforted me when I showed up at his strip club and started bawling like a baby, but I sort of figured he only did it because he felt sorry for me. Now he is hugging me again and I do not know what to make of it.

"Stop shakin' woman."

I snort. "Only you would command a person to stop shaking."

"It's going to be okay, Morgan. I know it doesn't seem that way now, but I promise it will be. I'll handle it."

I may not know much about Ice, but I believe he will handle the dead body and the now unconscious one I have just encountered.

I feel one of his hands move off of my back and then stroke over my hair once before he loosens his grip and steps away from me.

"Ride with me?"

"What?" My voice breaks.

"I'll take you home. Ride with me."

"On your motorcycle? What about my car?" My voice cracks with each sentence. I am drowning in emotion.

"I'll get a guy to come get your car."

"I've never ridden on a motorcycle."

"I'll be your first," he says with a wink.

He is my first—my first asshole.

"Now is hardly the time to flirt, joke, or be a smartass," I challenge him, letting my annoyance win over my instinct to be nice to everyone.

"I don't flirt. I don't joke. Telling me not to be a smartass is like telling you not to be cute. I am a smartass, jackass, and any other kind of ass there is." He tips my chin up to force me to meet his gaze. "Ride with me. Let go for just a bit and clear your head."

His plea is completely genuine. He truly wants to give me some peace in his own way. How do you turn a gesture like that down? The answer is, you don't. I give him an uncertain nod.

Why does it suddenly feel like I have bitten off way more than I can metaphorically chew?

ICE

Chapter
12

Ice

Damn girl, how did you get in them jeans?

That is the only thought rolling around in my head as I watch Morgan's hip sway with every step towards my bike. I want nothing more than to put my hand in the ass pocket of those jeans and squeeze that luscious ass.

What the hell is wrong with me? I seriously need to get laid. Morgan Powell is so far from my type of woman, but I can't shake her from my thoughts.

When Screech had given me the strange location her phone was tracked to, my heart stopped beating for a moment. My first reaction was to wonder whether she had been taken. Finding her here, seeking out her sister, pulls at something inside me.

I promise you, Madyson will come home. I won't fail. I won't let Morgan down. Somehow, I will find a way to give her everything she wants.

Pausing and taking in my own thoughts, it hits me. There is definitely more to what I feel for Morgan. I don't know how it happened or when, but she is drawing something out of me that I thought died the day Erin did.

As hard as this has been, she keeps pulling herself back together. She refuses to give up on her sister. Too bad the same can't be said for her parents.

The courage she possesses to face down some of the worst parts of town shows the depth of her character. She touched a damn dead body. I am sure it hasn't fully hit her yet, but it will. When it does, I have no doubt it will hurt, just as I know she will find a way to push it down and work through it.

I climb on my bike without giving another moment to my thoughts on Morgan. Kicking up the kickstand, I rock the bike up, popping the clutch with my foot and cranking the beast under me. When I turn my gaze to her, I see something longing in the depths of her beautiful green eyes.

"What?" I shout over the engine.

"I don't know what I'm doing," she shouts back uncertainly.

"What you're doing is getting on the bike." I extend my hand to her. Taking her shaking hand in mine, I tug her over to me and place her hand on my shoulder then nod my head down to the foot peg. She follows my thoughts and climbs on. Reaching behind me, I take both of her hands and wrap them firmly around my waist, pulling her against me. She is tense against me while her thighs squeeze mine, her head comes to rest on my shoulder, and her breath puffs on my neck in an erotic way that brings my cock to life.

"Do you trust me?" I ask, causing her to lift her head, bringing her lips against my ear.

"No," she firmly replies.

"Morgan, let it all go. I promise you, I'm doing everything I can for your sister. For the next half hour, be in this moment with me. Feel the wind around you, feel the power of the bike under you, and just live free with me."

She nods against me, her cheek brushing against my ear, causing my cock to press harder against my unforgiving zipper. As we pull off, the first jerk of the bike beneath her has her hands gripping my stomach tightly.

We travel down the road, and the scene to our right becomes the open beach filled with people who have not a care in the world. They lie out on their towels, not giving a second thought to the missing women. They aren't facing the challenge of keeping hope inside that their sister is still alive. No, they lie on the soft sand, letting their minds drift freely into whatever fantasy should decide to take root and grow there.

To our left is the hustle and bustle of the city businesses. People are shuffling around to get their souvenirs, their Cuban espressos, or get to their jobs. Whatever their purpose is today, they don't feel the pain and helplessness Morgan does right now.

I want some of this tranquility to seep into her. I know she is literally in knots, making herself sick over her sister, but she can't do this to herself. She has to keep from going insane while I look for Madyson. I know it seems hypocritical of me because, if anything like this ever happened to Brooke, I would tear the entire world down in a rage looking for her. I can't be worried about

Morgan slipping further away in despair while I am trying to find Madyson, though. I also can't afford to come save her from dangerous situations she unknowingly puts herself in.

Morgan may not trust me, but I am going to prove to her, one way or another, that she can. I am going to find Madyson if it is the last thing I do.

It takes her a bit before she finally relaxes behind me. Her hair whips around us both. Usually, this would bother me. I don't let many women ride bitch, and even less get to ride with their hair down, but with Morgan, all that matters to me is giving her this moment to have a release. I want nothing more than to liberate her from all her problems, if only for a little while. I can give her that.

A momentary escape.

A reprieve from unrealistic expectations.

A time to find herself, be herself, and not have to worry about anyone else.

I hope she takes it. There are times in my world where everything crashes down. Good men die, bad men live. People change, mistakes happen, and nothing is what it once was. My bike, the open road, and nothing except me along with the air around me are sometimes the only solid things I can find.

Dropping my left hand, I give her thigh a squeeze. Her grip on my waist tightens and her thighs come in closer to mine as she reacts to my touch.

Does she feel it? Even for a moment, can she find the release?

Morgan

We ride for what seems like hours, but in reality, it is only an hour to an hour and a half before Ice pulls up to his house.

As he cuts off the bike, I reluctantly unwrap myself from holding so tightly to his waist and drop my hands to his hips.

Somewhere along the ride, for just a little while, I forgot everything. I let myself be consumed by the salt in the air, my hair blowing freely in the wind, the rumble under me, and the man in front of me. Out on the road, the tension between Ice and me shifted. I gave him a piece of myself during that ride, whether he will ever realize it or not.

I took a part of him, as well. No matter what the future holds, I will forever be indebted to him for giving me a little sliver of peace. He allowed me a chance to get lost in the sensations around me, not remain stuck in my head. After this ride, I can see why women want this. There is a bond shared.

He sees inside of me. I don't know how he does it, but he does. Even when I didn't know I needed to breathe, to escape for only a little bit, he did, and he gave me that. He has asked me multiple times if I trust him. Until today and this ride together, my answer has been no. Now, I don't know if I would trust my darkest secrets with him—he is far from being my best friend—although

I do trust him to keep his word and to take care of everyone around him.

When he slaps my thigh gently to signal for me to climb off, I pause because I cannot seem to find a graceful way to remove myself from the bike. My legs feel like jelly. It takes some maneuvering before I manage to awkwardly climb off the bike and steady myself in his driveway.

Ice merely stares at me without moving or saying a word. Feeling insecure, I run my fingers through my hair, only to find it is more than a mess. From the knots, the texture, and the overall feel, I can only imagine it sticking out in every which way. No wonder I usually see women on bikes wearing braids. Great, now I can add this to the list of my weird moments with Ice. At least I am wearing jeans and a pair of Madyson's chucks. Otherwise, I would be really overdressed for our unexpected ride.

While I nervously roll back and forth on the balls of my feet as I stand before him, he blinks as if he is shaking off a daydream.

"Go on inside. Brooke can help you straighten out your hair and shit."

"I need my car so I can go home," I say quietly and nervously.

"You can stay here. Give me your keys and one of the boys will go get your car and deliver it to you. I doubt you want to be alone right now; stay here with Brooke. Plus, if you're here, I can keep track of you easier, and I don't have to stop searching for your sister to come get your ass from some ghetto."

"Oh, shit!" I exclaim, covering my mouth with my hand. "I didn't think you were really looking for her. I'm sorry." I didn't take it seriously that he would work to find her. Knowing he put a tracker on my phone shows he is more than serious, and although I am slightly ticked off that he was tracking me without my knowledge, I do understand it. Given my earlier encounter, I am even thankful for it.

"No apologies, not with me, ever. I take you as you are, and you get me as I am." Something flashes in his eyes, making me wonder if his words mean more than the here and now.

"What are your expectations?" I ask nervously, wondering what he wants me to do while he is looking for my sister.

"No expectations. They lead to resentments, as no one can ever measure up. You start with one set of expectations or requirements, and once someone meets those, the bar always gets raised."

"Let me rephrase then: what do you want me to do?"

"Trust me," he states simply, as if it is as easy as changing your panties in the morning. My face must have given away my skepticism because he asks, "You can't trust me?"

"I do trust you to try to find Madyson."

"Trust me to take care of you, too." He meets my gaze and extends his hand, making me feel like this is building up to something more than I am prepared for. With my small hand inside his large calloused one, he squeezes gently, and there is a monumental shift in the dynamic between us.

"Okay," I whisper back. "What do you need me to do?"

"Stay here until I get back. Hang out with Brooke. Do girlie shit. If you make some more of those cookies, I'll be sure to choke on them again." He winks.

I nod my head in agreement as he lets go of my hand. Reaching up, he tucks a piece of my tangled hair behind me ear. "Hang on, Morgan. I'll find her and the two of you will get through this."

He then starts the bike back up while I turn to walk inside. For the first time in days, I feel like everything will be all right. He will find my sister and bring her home. I feel it in my bones.

Chapter
13

Morgan

When I go into the house, I find Brooke sitting at the table, working on her homework. Feeling the need to do something, anything, I immediately head into the kitchen to bake, clean, or whatever else I can do to avoid sitting around and dwelling on my missing sister. Brooke takes notice of my presence as well as my need to fidget and gets up to join me.

"You know my dad will find her, right?"

"Sure," I say. I might have convinced myself earlier that Ice would find Madyson, but the doubts are starting to creep in. What if my confidence in Brooke's dad is wishful thinking?

"Seriously, Morgan. Things aren't always what they seem. My dad is one of the good guys, believe it or not."

"Your father's moral stature is not my business, Brooke. I don't know him well enough to make any assumptions as to whether he is good. The few interactions I've had with him haven't been so great, but again, I'm not his friend, nor am I his lover, so why should he afford me such things as the common decency of polite conversation?"

"He really is a different man than you think. I know he hasn't always been nice, but you aren't 'in there' with him yet."

"I don't think I want to be 'in there' with him, sweetie. No offense, but your dad is an ass," I state, raising my eyebrows at her.

"He's out right now looking for your sister, a girl that, in the grand scheme of things, doesn't even make his radar. He's put his entire club on the job to find Madyson and bring her home to you. Ever heard the saying, actions speak louder than words?" Brooke defends her father as fiercely as a mother lion would defend her cub. It is surprising and admirable.

"You are a wise one, Brooke Grady." I genuinely smile at her.

"Wise enough to know my dad put you on his bitch seat. That means something has changed."

"Huh?" I question, confused as she laughs at my reaction. "What's a bitch seat? And how does that change anything?"

"Rather than you bang around in the kitchen, let's go get you a hair tie, hair brush, and some serious detangling spray. Once we do something about your hair, I'll clue you in on biker life."

Taking me by the hand, she drags me to her bathroom, which frankly, anyone who isn't blind would be able to tell is Brooke's bathroom. The entire room is decorated in fuchsia pink, purple, and black. It is bright enough for me to *wish* I was blind. It makes me wonder if

Ice is able to step in here without breaking out into some sort of hives.

Brooke sits me down on a chair in front of her vanity, and when I finally look up into the mirror, I gasp and cringe in horror. My hair is tangled and trying to stick up in every direction. It almost looks as if a couple of birds attacked my head and tried to make a nest out of it. I wonder if it would be easier to cut it all off instead of trying to detangle it.

I almost tell Brooke to forget it, that we will drive to the closest hair stylist to shave my head bald, but I look up and see her determined face. She has a bottle of hair detangling spray in one hand and a wide tooth comb in the other. Fifteen minutes later, I am absolutely positive that this young girl has had entirely too much practice fixing women's motorcycle hair gone wrong.

A small part of me starts to wonder if Brooke has had to do this for some of the women Ice has shared his bed with, though I cut the thought off quickly. Part of me knows, without a doubt, that Ice would not bring women home to meet his daughter. It is obvious the man goes out of his way to protect her, and I would assume it includes limiting that aspect of his life to her, as well.

Furthermore, why should I care about Brooke detangling the hair of any woman Ice might bring home? He is not my man, and he never will be. As such, it is none of my business if he does bring a woman home.

Grabbing my hand, the sweet and adorable daughter of the hard-ass biker who seems to haunt me, drags me out of the bathroom and back towards the front of the house. "Now that I can look at you and not want to laugh, let's go to the living room and have some girl talk."

We sit down beside each other on the couch, and a sadness creeps over Brooke almost instantly. "I miss her like crazy, you know. I get this has to be crazy hard for you because it's crazy hard for me, too."

I have been so wrapped up in my own hurt and fear that I have completely forgotten how my sister going missing might affect her best friend. "Yes, sweetie, it is. We have to keep holding on to hope that she will come home soon."

"I don't want to scare you, but I don't believe she ran away. Madyson may be a little crazy, but underneath it all, she has goals and aspirations. She wants to do so much in the future. She wouldn't risk not graduating."

My heart hurts a little more at Brooke now defending my sister the way she has her father. It is obvious this girl knows more about Madyson than I might ever know, if Ice is unable to find her. That realization burns. It is a stark reminder that I should have done more for my little sisters growing up. I should have tried harder to get to know then instead of pasting on a fake smile and doing whatever I had to do to appease the adults.

"Mady and I aren't all that close, Brooke. With her living with me, this is the most she's ever let me in," I finally reply sadly.

"She wants to be a marine biologist. She even has two partial scholarships for college lined up. They aren't much, but it's something. We only have one class together this semester, but we had two last. She studies hard. She doesn't even get into trouble at school."

"How do you have classes with her if you're a junior?"

"I'm kind of a nerd, I guess. I'm one of the smart kids. My dad is an ass, and if I don't bring home straight A's, he'll ground me. Dad's version of grounding is torture. He takes everything away, and I mean *everything*. I'm not allowed to leave my room, a room he takes down to the bare essentials. He literally leaves me with four empty walls, a bed, and a dresser with my clothes set out to the ugliest outfits I own. No TV, no books that aren't school related, no fashion shows, nothing. I get nothing.

"Hell, once he took all my makeup away. He said it was because I was spending too much time 'primping' and not enough time studying. Truth is, I think he can't handle me wearing makeup and growing up. Mady and I have been trying to be more social; that's why we went to the parties. Kids at school are afraid of the Regulators, and Mady doesn't want to bring anyone around your parents."

Shifting in my spot, I turn to look her in the eyes. "You know fitting in isn't all that important in the grand scheme of life, right? High school passes and life begins. What any of those people in school think of you or my sister doesn't matter."

Brooke's eyebrows furrow a little and she grouses, "We know that. Still, it would be fun to be popular."

"I suppose it would, but at what cost? Mady was drugged at the last party. What if you had been, too?

Then you wouldn't have been able to save either one of you," I chide her gently.

"I guess I didn't think of that."

"Look, my parents are superficial. There are a lot of things they've done that I don't agree with. But the thing is, my upbringing made me who I am today, and I'm okay with me. I may not be one of the 'cool' people, but I have a great job, solid income, and I have a good foundation for my future. The people around me love me for me, faults and all. Surround yourself with people who accept the nerdy you, like Mady. Find people who aren't scared off by your biker dad, if that's even possible. Most importantly, be you and love you just as you are."

"Madyson always said that about you," Brooke whispers.

"What did she say?" I need some reassurance that I have been a positive influence on my sister somehow, because I feel like I have failed her in every other aspect.

"Even though you did a lot of things just to keep your parents quiet, you always find happiness in whatever situation you're in. She looks up to you."

My eyes sting with tears threatening to build. "I don't know what to say." Really, I don't. I am not happy. Have I put on the façade for so long no one can see through to the real me? I can't say I am unhappy, though. What I am is lonely.

We talk for a little while longer. Brooke has some great memories with her grandmother. It hurts my heart to know she has no memories of her own mother. My heart aches to have more time with her and to do things like this with my sisters.

Madyson, when you get back, we are going to have quality time together. I am going to know all about your dreams and be there to help you make them come true.

Ice

"Are you sure it's her?" I ask Screech as I stare at the screen in front of me. For two very long days we have had a man watching the four cameras.

"Her tattoo—"

"Tattoo, what tattoo? She's a damn kid," I bark out.

"Apparently, she had a friend tattoo a Japanese cherry blossom on her side with her initials weaved into it. Her file states that it was done a little over a year ago."

"Do we have a location yet?" Hammer asks the most important question.

I stare at the vision before me of Madyson Leigh Powell, naked and slumped down in a cage. She is moving; at least I know she is alive. Has she mentally checked out? How drugged is she? Have they violated her yet?

My stomach turns at the thought that this case is hitting a little too close to home. Staring at my baby girl's best friend exposed, defenseless, and probably scared out of her mind makes me think an ugly truth that I do not want to face. *That could easily have been Brooke, instead.*

From what we have gathered, it takes a while before they start using the girls for sex. They spend the first parts of their captivity being drugged to the point of addiction. Once they have them hooked, the bastards whore them out. Consensual my ass. Sick fucks have a system going. How Madyson caught their radar, however, we are still unsure. It seems like it was a matter of wrong place, wrong time.

A man approaches her cage, syringe in hand. We all watch helplessly in horror as he unlocks the door. When Madyson scurries into the corner of her enclosure as if she could somehow be swallowed up by the ground and hide, the man reaches out and grabs her leg. She shakes her head back and forth, hitting the sides of the cage. She kicks out, and he yanks on her harshly, causing her head to bang on the back of the enclosure. Unable to do anything except watch as she is drugged against her will, anger boils inside me like never before.

"I will kill every single one of these fuckers slowly, painfully, and with vengeance for every single needle they have injected into each one of these women," I state to the room coldly.

I watch as her body relaxes, and then the man tosses her leg back inside and closes the door. She is unmoving, unresponsive, and I can only send up a prayer that she will wake up after whatever is in her system passes through.

"Are you gonna tell Morgan that we found her?" Hammer asks.

I shake my head no.

"If it were Brooke, you would want to know. You would want the hope and knowledge that she is still breathing," Coal remarks.

"For how long, huh? I can't promise her we will make it in time if we can't lock in on a location soon. She can't handle this." I let my irritation show.

Hammer snorts. "She can't handle it, or you can't handle the possibility of letting her down? How do you know she can't cope? How do you know this isn't the shred of hope she needs to keep going? She's never had to face anything like this."

"I can't fail her or Madyson," I say, meeting my brother's stare.

"You won't. Morgan is tough. She didn't hesitate to take in her sister. She doesn't back down from you, and you're a scary motherfucker. She can handle this. Honestly, she is one of only a handful of women that could be strong knowing what we do."

"What are you getting at, Hammer?"

"Just saying she's different."

"This is a conversation best suited for a different time," I state as my agitation grows. I don't need to stand around talking about Morgan when I need to find these trapped women.

"Agreed," Hammer replies. "The conversation will happen, though, at a better time."

I nod my head, knowing he is as stubborn as a mule. He is locked onto this, there is no changing his mind.

"We need a plan. We need a solid headcount. As soon as we have a lock on their location, we're going in. Fuck the FBI and any other jackass in a uniform. I'm not waitin' around. When we have a definite spot, we're engaging. We need Crissy to get something set up for the girls, and Doc will need to be on stand-by."

The guys all nod their heads in agreement as they mentally get in the zone for what we will need after we recover the captured women.

"Vans, we'll need multiple vans. This isn't going to sound fair or nice, but damn, we gotta be safe," Skid pipes in with a disgusted look on his face. "We need to cover the cages and transport the girls out that way."

Coal looks darkly at our brother.

"Hear me out," Skid adds, taking note of his reaction. "We don't know if the needles have been shared. Some of these women were users before getting kidnapped. Now they've been whored out, too. Before we risk getting scratched, bitten, or otherwise attacked, I think we need to be smart."

Coal pushes off from the table and turns to stare at the wall. Without looking at them, I know none of the men in the room like having to put Coal through this mission. It is bringing too much up from his twisted past. Although his circumstances were different, aspects of this case are close enough to what happened when he was younger to fuck with his head. I wish I had time to sit my brother down, talk to him about it like I probably should have done a long time ago; however, we don't have time for it now.

"I get it, Coal. We need to be safe, though. Once we get them to the safe house, slowly, one by one, we can release them. This is different than anything we've done in the past. This is ten times the amount of packages to be picked up and delivered to safety from a hostile zone we're infiltrating. Add to that an unknown amount of guards, and the level of danger further escalates. As much as I don't like it, Skid's right.

"Think about it. We're going into hostile territory, which means getting in and out quickly. We don't have the time to be fighting with half drugged women who could be infected with AIDS, for crying out loud. I don't like the idea of traumatizing them any more than you do, but I don't want to get scratched by a hysterical woman and end up with a disease, either. We gotta be smart. You fuckin' know this."

"Knowin' it doesn't make it any easier," Coal answers, blowing out a breath.

"Nothin' about what we do is ever easy," Hammer says as a sober silence fills the room. We can all see a woman, three cages down from Madyson, is having a seizure.

"Find the damn location, Screech!" I roar before slamming my fist into the wall, causing two of his monitors to fall and shatter. I don't care. All of this equipment is nothing but a useless pile of junk if we can't find the source of the feeds.

ICE

Chapter
14

Ice

Getting home, I am kicking myself for being so late. I walk into my living room and find Morgan asleep in my chair, the remote on the floor by her feet. I loudly move around in the hope she will wake up. She can sleep in the guest room, but I don't want to be the one to move her.

Going in the kitchen, I find a note on the counter.

Your dinner plate is in the microwave. Dessert is a chocolate mousse in the fridge. You shouldn't choke on that. ~M~

I smile at her attitude, even in a letter. This woman challenges me in a way I have never been tested.

After eating my dinner and dessert, I clean up the kitchen, again loudly. When I arrive back in the living room, she hasn't moved.

Damn. She must sleep like the dead. I haven't managed to sleep like that since before basic training. A man learns to keep one ear open and run on little sleep when his life could depend upon it. Still, it does something to me to see her sleeping so soundly in my house after I know how she has run herself into the ground the last several days worrying over her sister.

Scooping her up, I start to take her into the guest room; however, I look down and see the tear lines, she has obviously been crying tonight. With as tired as Morgan's been, I do not want to leave her sleeping in a chair that might hurt her neck and back. I also do not like the idea of putting her in the guest room, because I know the mattress is not in the best shape anymore and can be uncomfortable to sleep on. The woman is dog tired and deserves a good night's sleep. There is only one available bed in the house left, and that is in my room. It means giving up my own bed for the night, but it won't kill me to sleep on a shitty mattress. I have slept on far worse in my Army days. Therefore, I follow my instincts and make my way up the stairs to my room with her.

Tucking her into my bed, I then wait for her to wake up and want to leave, to protest being in my room. The prickly woman would probably apologize for 'invading my space' or some crazy shit. It doesn't happen, though; so I strip down to my boxer briefs and get ready to crash in the guest room myself.

I am heading out of the room when she moves and begins mumbling in her sleep. I know I should keep going, but I can't. There is an undeniable pull inside me towards her. Following my gut, I make my way over and climb in bed beside her. As if it was second nature, she moves over to me in the bed and snuggles into me. I don't have any choice except to wrap my arm around her or be miserable for the few hours of sleep I would like to try to get.

It is a strange feeling to have a woman in my bed to merely sleep. I have not had anyone share my bed without having sex since Erin. My young mind never grasped that there could come a time that I wouldn't be able to have my arm around my wife in the moments lost to peaceful slumber. Then life happened, and she was ripped cruelly from me.

After feeling that sort of pain, I never wanted another woman completely entrenched in my heart. Now, here I lie with another woman sleeping in my arms, and I feel the same sort of peace wash over me that I have not felt in far too long. Furthermore, it doesn't feel like a betrayal to Erin, not that I want to analyze that realization right now.

Morgan's breaths tickle my bare chest as she continues her trip through oblivion. My mind wanders, and I whisper quietly into the night to my dead wife.

"Erin, what am I doing? Things are changing. I have given things to Morgan Powell that I didn't think I had in me to ever give again."

There is no response, just like every other time I have allowed my mind to reach out for her.

Morgan's hand comes across my waist much like Erin used to do, and her gentle touch soothes something in me. Her legs tangle in mine as if she is wrapping me in the security of her cocoon. Like a caterpillar being safely surrounded during a change, I am being given a soft, safe, and secure place to let my heart change, open, and fall.

Before I can think further on where any of this is happening, I fall asleep.

"Oh, my goodness, no way."

I wake up to a frantic Morgan pushing up off me. Her hair is a tousled, sexy mess around her face, and her eyes are not quite focused yet. Some women are only pretty when they put time into make-up and doing their hair. Now I get the chance to see that this woman is gorgeous fresh faced in the morning.

"I am *so* sorry. I haven't slept well since Madyson disappeared, only a few hours here and there when I pass out from exhaustion. Oh, my… I'm just so sorry."

"I'm not," I state honestly while my dick starts to stir. I am not sure if I should start doing algebra to stop it or say fuck it and let it happen.

She looks at me intently, as if she is trying to gage the depth of my sincerity. I watch her back, wondering if I should kiss her, whether she will pull that stick out of her uptight ass and let me. Before we can discuss or do anything, my bedroom door flies open.

"What the hell? I like her dad. I really like her. Why?" Brooke screams in her teenage hysteria. When she is like this, I feel like it is DEFCON level five or some shit. I am never going to understand hormonal, teenage girls. This sort of shit makes me want to grab my helmet along with my guns and head to a fucking bunker to hide.

Morgan's face pales as my eyes grow wild at my daughter's assumption.

"I can talk to Morgan. Finally, since Gram, I have someone to talk to. Now you've fucked her and fucked it all up," Brooke yells, her eyes watering with unshed tears before turning to stomp downstairs.

"I'm so sorry, Ice. This is all my fault. God, I don't even know your first name, and your daughter thinks we had sex." Morgan moves to climb out of bed.

"It's okay. I'll handle it. And my name is Brett." I can't help smiling at her mortification. The way she says sex is like a teen who just completed health class. It is cute, exactly like everything else about Morgan.

"No. Please, let me. I don't want her to think this is more than it is."

"You want to face the battle of a teenage girl hell bent on ripping someone's balls off? Feel free. If you need to wave the white flag, I'll be down after I shower to take over," I answer grumpily, not liking her comment about this not being more than what it is. I am used to barflies falling all over themselves to have a piece of me. Then the first woman who manages to chip though some of this barrier I have thrown up since Erin died is practically running after my daughter to assure her we would never have sex. That is enough to do a man's ego in.

Before she leaves, she smiles at me—really, truly smiles. It is something I haven't seen from her before, and it is abso-fucking-lutely exquisite. She is a masterpiece of natural beauty, both inside and out.

Damn, I may be in over my head with more than just my daughter.

Morgan

Making my way nervously down to the kitchen, I find Brooke pouring milk into a bowl of cereal. There is an awkward silence between us while she obviously fights herself to not look at me.

Approaching cautiously, I say, "I promise you I didn't have sex with your dad."

Her head comes up, and her eyes meet my gaze. "I woke up and expected to find you downstairs. Finding you in his bed… I don't know. You're both adults, so it's not like my business, or whatever," she stammers in frustration.

"Anything with your dad is your business. You need to learn a better way to communicate with him, though. I enjoy talking to you, and I wouldn't do anything with your dad behind your back. Honestly, your dad and I are complete opposites, sweetie. I don't even make his radar." I have never had to explain myself like this before. I hope I am doing it considerately enough because I would never want to come between Brooke and her father.

"I've heard him and the guys talk about his revolving door of barflies. And I even walked in on him like twice with one of them. I don't want that for you, Morgan," she whispers.

The mention of Ice's reputation hurts. Waking up in the man's arms was very surreal yet very nice, too. For that minute, when I was somewhere in between asleep and awake, I felt safe and protected. Not quite loved, though maybe something close. I know it was only my overactive imagination, but damn, it felt nice to have that for a little while. Maybe it is for the best that I received this little reality check before my mind has a chance to get ahead of itself.

"I'm so far from being like that with your dad. Heck, I don't even know that we're friends, truth be told. He's just helping me find Mady. Last night, I was tired, and I guess I ended up in his bed, though I have no idea how. I haven't been sleeping well, I crashed. I can't believe I'm going to say this, but"—I facetiously gasp and move my hand dramatically to my chest—"I think he was trying to be nice to me. Can you believe that?" Leaning in to conspiratorially whisper, I ask, "Should we call the news and tell them the world is ending?"

We both fall into a fit of giggles, and for a moment, I don't feel like the weight of the world is on my shoulders. For just a moment, I get lost in being an over-the-top, silly woman.

Brooke's giggles die slowly. Then she looks me over and bites her bottom lip, as if she is unsure she should say what she is thinking. "He is a good guy. He doesn't allow himself to get into a serious relationship with anyone, though. He's only let me know the name of one woman, in the thirteen years since my mom died."

I let her words sink in for a moment. "Brooke, you know you mean everything to him, right?"

"Sure," she replies with a sarcastic smirk.

"Hear me out. The man has made sure to have a system in place so that, at all times, he knows you are safe and taken care of. You are his first and last priority. I get that you think he's a playboy or whatnot, and that may be the case, but he obviously tries to shelter you from that if you don't know their names. Men have needs; he can't hide that. He sets the bar high for the women he allows to be around you; obviously, since you have only officially met one of them."

"Truth," Ice's voice calls from behind me. "Brooke, nothing happened with Morgan. Don't question it further, and don't ever throw your attitude around like that again, or I'll ground your ass until graduation."

"Dad," she whines.

"Brooke, show some respect. You may not agree with what your dad says or does, but he takes care of you, and he loves you. The two of you have to find a balance, and no more yelling on either side," I say with a sharp stare back over to Ice.

My parents are far from being a good example, but they never yell. I have been trained in the way to firmly communicate an order without raising my voice.

"Never ceases to amaze me. She can handle what my teen throws out," Ice mumbles as he brushes past me. He kisses Brooke on the top of her head before going to the coffee pot.

Not being certain that he was actually talking to me, I blankly stare at the man in front of me. His low slung sweat pants only accentuate the clearly defined muscles of his body. The pants barely stay above his butt, which is both firm looking and also nice and round. For the first time in my life, I have the overwhelming urge to grab a man's ass, and it disturbs me; as a result, I focus on another body part in the hopes that the sensation will go away.

Moving my gaze over his flexing triceps, my eyes widen a bit as I realize the man's arms are huge. I swear his biceps are bigger than my thighs. The intricate work of his tattoos draws me in. I can't exactly make out what is on his upper arm without moving in closer, but it looks as if it is some sort of skull wearing a green beret.

With his back to me, I am able to take in the large tattoo that covers it. A large eagle with his wings out on display holds a sword in his grasp. Above the eagle's head in bold letters is the word 'REGULATORS'. As he moves around, filling the coffee pot with water and ground coffee, the muscles in his back ripple. In all my life, I have never analyzed a man's body enough to know they could be built in such a way, and now I realize I have been missing out. Backs built like Ice's are sort of beautiful and might just be my new favorite body part.

"Morgan's gonna stay here until we get Madyson back," Ice states matter-of-factly while pushing the button on the pot to brew. I seriously need more than coffee to take in what he just said.

"Excuse me?" I question, flabbergasted while Brooke simply smiles. "I thought I was only staying for the night!"

"You haven't been sleeping well. Stay here so you can feel safe and not be lost in your thoughts. Brooke will talk your head off and be a good distraction." He gets his coffee cup out, sets in on the counter, and then continues to move around the kitchen as if ordering me and my life around is an everyday feat for him.

"You make it sound so simple. I have a home of my own, ya know."

"Save the Ms. Independent bullshit for when your sister comes home. For now, you need to eat. As much as I like fitness, I like a woman with curves, and sweetheart, your curves are disappearin'. We can't have that. It would be fuckin' criminal to let that ass of yours waste away. You need to sleep. You also need to let me do my job, and part of doing my job means looking out for you, too. I can do that better if you're in my house. Your car is in the garage with a remote opener in the console. Take Brooke, get some shit, and settle in."

What the hell just happened?

Somehow, I feel as if I have been pulled in a little more into Ice's world when I barely finished promising Brooke I would stay firmly away.

Chapter
15

Ice

I should have kept my ass upstairs. Watching Morgan handle Brooke with kindness, compassion, understanding while remaining firm—damn, just damn. I am a man who can recognize a good woman, and Morgan Powell is a good fucking woman. Too good for me.

Do I send her away? Nope. I love to torture myself with exactly what I want yet can't have.

My phone rings, providing me the exact escape I need from the estrogen filled kitchen. After too much time around Morgan Powell, I feel the need to reach down, grab my dick, and make sure I still have my balls. Not that I am too worried about her giving me sass. The woman likes to throw her no nonsense prim and proper attitude around when she feels the need to get bossy; however, that doesn't mean I will stand here and take it.

She may have enough attitude to try and tell me off, but I have no problem with simply throwing her over my shoulder and finding some really creative ways to show her who holds the reigns around here. The problem is, I shouldn't want to get that sort of creative with her. That sort of creative means naked body parts, time with her, and me caring about showing her just how much of a man I am. Therein lies the problem—caring means I am getting attached. I have no business caring for a woman like her.

Fuck, what have I gotten myself into?

Making my way out into the backyard, I answer the blocked call. "Ice."

"Good morning, compañero de negocios," Sandoval greets through the phone.

"What?"

"Word has it that you are looking to expand your options in your house of whores." The greed he has is evident in every word.

"Possibly. I have room for more should an opportunity present itself. The last girls we got are working out well," I lie. We are still trying to sort out the women's identities. They were hooked on the drugs so long the detox almost killed them. Their memories are fuzzy at best, for the time being, and patience is a virtue, one I don't have. In my line of work, it is both a blessing and a curse.

"Three more. Price is the same. Meet me tonight at the hangar, ten sharp." He disconnects the call without another word.

This is just the break we have needed.

Rushing inside, I try to push aside the laughter I hear from my daughter only a few rooms away. When is the last time she really relaxed and laughed? Clearly, she doesn't do this enough. Making a mental note to work on this, I continue to my room to get dressed while making a call for the boys to come in for sermon.

A quick change, goodbyes, and I am out the door in less than fifteen minutes. Arriving at the bat cave, I have everyone waiting on me.

"Sandoval is ready to do more business. We get three girls tonight. Screech, get on it. Track every single one of those fuckers we can. All damn day. They have to pick the girls up from the warehouse."

"On it, Ice," he replies while clicking madly on his keyboard. The screen switches from the live feed of the girls to a map with blinking lights for each phone he has a lock on already.

"He just made the wrong move in his very own game," Coal says with a smirk.

The adrenaline in the air rises with each moment shared between me and my boys. We are so close; we can't fuck it up now with a hasty decision. It is time to get prepared for war, something each and every man in this room is more than familiar with.

"Prep time. Meet me in the armory," I order.

"Checkmate, motherfucker," Hammer says, heading out the door to do what he does best—ready our weapons and load up.

The day passes in a whirlwind of checking and double checking our weapons. We know tonight is a make it or break it meeting with Sandoval. If all goes well, we will buy three more girls from the man we are now confident is behind the missing women and pinpoint where he is holding the others. If Screech can give us that information, we will launch a mission tomorrow to rescue the remaining women.

When night finally falls, we arrive at the hangar five minutes early. All except two of my men come with me. Inside, three of Sandoval's men are waiting for us. One of them speaks into a walkie-talkie, and it is an easy guess that he is informing his boss of our arrival because, a mere minute later, Sandoval walks in from the hangar's back door.

Me and every one of my men are on edge tonight. For them, it is because they know we are close enough to the end of this job. They can almost taste victory. For me, it is because I know that, if everything goes well, I will be bringing Madyson home to Morgan and Brooke tomorrow.

Just because we are ready to end Sandoval, does not mean we are cocky, though. If anything, we are that much more vigilant to any move, threat, or possibility that could put our mission in jeopardy.

All of us are ready to end this fucker.

The hangar is no different tonight than any other night. Although Sandoval should change up his meeting locations, I have information showing he has some of the patrolling officers of the area on his payroll. Add to it being privately owned, and you get the result that the security checks are scheduled rather than random. Lazaro Sandoval may have made his biggest mistake in finally becoming too comfortable.

With his trademark smarmy smile, Sandoval strides slowly over to me. "Your asere here is insatiable, no?" He glances over to Coal and gives him a wink. Referring to my brother as insatiable whether in Spanish or English is so far from the truth.

My VP may be a seasoned warrior, but a man can only take so much before he snaps. I don't want to take the chance that Sandoval's ribbing pushes Coal beyond his limits.

Shrugging to our seller, I reply nonchalantly, "What can I say, I like to keep my men in pussy. If I take care of them, they'll take care of me."

"Damn right we will, boss," Hammer says. "So, where are the goods? My boys are ready to have a little party tonight to break them in." He rubs his hand over his dick through his jeans to illustrate his point.

Sandoval barks a laugh, shaking his head in amusement. "I thought about asking your Vice President for another show since the last one was so enjoyable. Any man who can take two women like that knows what he is doing, yes? Unfortunately, there is no free time for such pleasurable activities tonight. So, down to business it is."

Raising his hand, he signals his man by the back hangar door who lifts his walkie-talkie and speaks into it. A few seconds later, the door once again opens, this time to reveal three women wearing nothing more than lingerie and heels. They are all drugged and wobbling so badly that, even with the help of the men escorting them in a relentless hold by their upper arms, they still struggle to walk.

"See? I gift wrapped them for you this time," Sandoval laughs.

One of the women abruptly stumbles and crashes to land on the floor on her hands and knees. My chest squeezes a little as I watch her whimper in pain, but I stay stock still as if totally uncaring for her predicament.

Sandoval spits out some rapid fire commands to his men in his native tongue that I can't understand, but the message is clear. He is not happy that the merchandise almost hurt herself before delivery.

One of the men roughly picks up the crying woman with one hand in her hair and the other on her arm. The unhappy Cuban drags her the rest of the way to us, ignoring her screams, until he throws her at Hammer, who manages to catch her just before she falls again.

Unable to soothe the frightened woman, I watch as Hammer throws her over his shoulder and smacks a hand over her ass when she starts to struggle. It is time to wrap this negotiation up before anything else is said or done that can set one of my men off.

Reaching back blindly, I reach my hand out for the bag of money Roy Boy is holding for me. Once it is handed over, I throw it at the dipshit that is standing next to Sandoval.

"Here's your payment. Thanks for our party toys."

The lackey opens the bag, quickly counts the money, and then gives his boss the signal that it is all there.

"It is good to do business with you once again, Ice. I look forward to your next order."

I give him a chin lift when, honestly, I would rather give him a few bullet holes in that fuck-ugly face of his. Turning around, my boys and I walk out, though with our instincts on high alert to make sure we are not attacked from behind as we leave.

Once we get the women settled in with Doc and Crissy, we make a quick rendezvous back to Screech.

"Location found. Specs of surrounding area being determined now," Screech immediately spouts off when we enter the room.

"Skid, BJ, Hammer, you're on extraction points. Coal, you'll ready the boxes. Rocks, make sure Crissy and Doc are ready for the rest of the women. Screech, have you tallied a rough count for us on how many they have?"

"Currently, we have seventeen in that particular facility."

"He may have sold off some like he did with us, which I'm guessing is the most likely option since the Ex Ops Team found one of the missing women down in Mexico at the Rivera Cartel's stronghold. He probably didn't want to keep merchandise on hand for too long. Some may have died from the drugs or other unknown medical conditions. Or he may have another location," Hammer replies, knowing the numbers don't add up to cover all the missing women.

We spend the next two hours ironing out our plans for the next day. On any mission, you have a plan A, a plan B if shit starts to go south, and plan C, which is light up all your tangos and haul ass back to the extraction point because everything is FUBAR.

After securing our weapons, acknowledging our entry and exit points, we are ready to head home. I check in on Madyson on the screen one last time before leaving.

"Hang tight. I'll get you home to your sister soon," I say to the screen.

Adrenaline courses through me knowing that tomorrow is the day.

Arriving home, I struggle to wind down. When I enter the kitchen, the smell of cinnamon assaults my nose. My kitchen never smells this good.

"Fuckin' cookies," I say to myself with a smile. "Bakin' fuckin' cookies."

"You know something?" Morgan asks, entering the space.

"You should be asleep." I answer to avoid her question.

Morgan shakes her head, and I can see the faint tremble of her lip. "I can't sleep knowing she's out there, possibly hurt, sick, or someone doing things to her."

Seeing the tears well up in her eyes, I go over and take her in my arms. She wraps around me in an embrace that feels like second nature somehow. She fits into me.

I hold her for a while, running my hands through her hair, neither of us saying a word. She doesn't question me further, and I don't offer any answers.

Morgan

Feeling myself being lifted, I start to wake up. My mind is fuzzy as I remember sitting on the couch, snuggled into Ice. After our moment in the kitchen, he wanted to eat and then watch TV. I joined him, and I guess I finally dozed off.

Opening my eyes, I see he is carrying me to his room, not the guest room.

"I can walk, you know," I whisper.

"Always sassy, aren't you? It's more fun this way."

"This isn't the guest room," I point out as he lays me on his bed.

"You aren't a regular guest," he replies with a chuckle.

"Yeah, I guess I should pay rent, huh?" I playfully give him his own words back.

"I was an ass," he replies while he makes his way into his overly large closet and out of my sight.

"Yup, you are an ass."

"I heard that. Go to sleep." I hear him moving around and apparently changing clothes.

"Always so bossy. Where are you going?"

He emerges in black cargo pants, a snug black T-shirt that I swear should be painted on, and a shoulder holster with a gun secured in place. He looks like an assassin bad boy out of a Hollywood movie—scary and sexy all rolled into one sinfully delicious package.

"Sweetheart, you have no idea how bossy I am. I have some work to do. I don't know when I'll be home. Keep an eye on Brooke, and I'll be in touch."

Something in his eyes, his demeanor—I am not sure exactly what, but it tells me his work today involves my sister. There has been a change between us.

I don't know why or what exactly overcomes me, but I quickly hop out of bed and make my way to him.

Looping my arms around his waist, I roll up on my tiptoes and tentatively brush my lips against his. I don't know what I am doing; I simply let my instincts run me.

Boldly, I open my mouth ever so slightly, and with the tip of my tongue, I trace the seam of his lips. For the first time, I taste the essence that is the man who both confuses and arouses me. He growls against my mouth for a second, the vibration feeling as though it runs through my entire body.

Both of his hands come up to grab either side of my head when he finally gives in. The dynamic shifts rapidly from a sweet kiss to a passion-filled, lust-controlled demand. I am no longer in control as Ice ravages my mouth. It makes me wonder if he would ravage the rest of my body with such a sensual ferocity.

Our tongues dance while he seems to devour every crevice. His hands roam my body, causing me to moan as he squeezes my ass. I have never been kissed with such longing before, such need. I have never known a man could make a woman feel this out of control with such an animalistic hunger. My body melts helplessly against him as I become a ball of mush, giving in to my every desire.

As suddenly as I began our kiss, he is pulling away. Pushing me away from him, he makes sure I am steady on my feet before brushing one last kiss across my forehead.

"Get some sleep," he orders before exiting the room without a look back.

What the hell just happened? Every encounter with this man seems to leave me asking myself this.

Yet, I still don't have any damn answers.

ICE

Chapter
16

Ice

From the camera views, we expected to enter a warehouse since one may consider the space storage of some sort. Really, what the operation is set up in is an old hotel that has long since closed down. It is now considered a storage facility for a nearby deluxe spa for recovering patients of the same plastic surgeon who owns the hangar Sandoval uses for his transactions.

Apparently, Lazaro Sandoval spreads his money out to cover all his operations under the guise of truly legitimate commerce. Smart man. This is one of the reasons he has lasted as long as he has in such a brutal and unforgiving business.

After spending the night doing final preparations, we have men in place on the surrounding buildings' rooftops. No one will exit the building and stay alive unless they are carried out by us. One might think broad day light wouldn't be the time to do this; however, Sandoval has fewer men on guard during this time. Perhaps he thinks no one is bold enough to attack him then. Whatever his reasoning, it is an advantage we can't ignore.

The location of the feeds narrowed the women to a service room for janitorial supplies, which has an underground parking garage next to it where we are able to drive the vans right inside. We can see the cameras as we enter, but Screech has scrambled their feed. Once he got a lock on the location, he was able to hack in and control their system. They have no guard on the garage because it would arouse suspicion on the building. Another mistake on their part that I plan to take full advantage of.

The biggest concern we have is that there is only one way in and one way out. Without the ability to exit from a different point, it creates a kill box that makes it easy for your target to pick you off one by one as you try to come and go. This means we will have to stay vigilant while we move through the building.

We have learned they were using the service elevator to bring the girls up to the hotel rooms to service the clients; therefore, Screech scrambled the upstairs cameras, as well. Once the men inside realize all of the cameras are not functioning, they are going to spread throughout the building looking for trouble, and my men and I are ready to show them plenty.

Exiting the four vans, Coal and his team of five ready to make the assent using the stairwells to seek out any victims upstairs. Our intel shows Sandoval runs his operation from his office on the third floor. Knowing his God complex, we don't expect there to be anyone on the couple of floors above him, but we have already discussed Coal and his team double checking them to be sure.

Hammer and his team spread out to surround the garage. He will be on stand-by to assist Coal if he gets upstairs and finds more people than we visually confirmed on the feeds. Otherwise, as we evacuate the girls, he will direct and aid in loading the vans. Once full, he and his team will take the vans out and switch to our back up vehicles to keep the flow of rescued girls continuous.

Throwing my arm up in a ninety degree angle, I hold up my fist in the stand by position as I ready myself for whatever may greet me on the other side of the metal door in front of me. Knowing there will be a barrage of bullets once they realize we are here, I say a silent prayer our Kevlar vests will do their jobs. I have a little girl I have every intention of going home to today, and I don't plan on bringing home any of my guys in body bags.

My chest rises and falls as I listen intently through the outside of the door for any signs that Sandoval's guys are clued in to us. Thankfully, I hear nothing abnormal, only a couple of muffled voices.

Giving Screech the low affirmative that we are in position, he begins our countdown. *Five*. I feel my men tense up behind me. *Four*. Readying themselves to head into action. *Three*. Inhale deeply. *Two*. Exhale slowly. *One*. It's go time.

I give the signal to my men to move in and place my hand on my gun while Skid moves to open the door. As soon as the door opens enough to allow me entrance, I move through it, ready to face anyone who might be on the other side with Coal and Big Jim right behind me. Coal moves on to his part of our mission, while Big Jim helps me engage our enemy.

Immediately, the guards jump up on the other side of the room where they were lazily sitting around a table.

They reach for their weapons in a scramble, but I won't give them a chance to save their own sorry asses. I fire off shots in rapid succession as we fully enter the room, trying to aim high to avoid hitting one of the victims in the cages, which are on the floor between us and our targets.

Simultaneously, as Big Jim and I lay down cover fire, Coal and his team move to the stairwell on our immediate left. They disappear as silently as wraiths up the stairs in an attempt to surprise anyone above them.

My focus never moves off the men in front of me as part of my team rushes in through the door behind us. Moving forward, I remain focused on our targets.

We manage to take two of the four guards out quickly while the other two duck for cover. Dipshit number one tries to hide behind a concrete pillar. The few girls not drugged beyond oblivion cry out in fear, although most of them are tucked in the corners of their cages, unresponsive to the chaos. Dipshit number two has crouched behind one of the crates, using a helpless woman for a shield. By the frantic movements of his hands, I can tell his clip has jammed, giving me the opportunity to move in on him. Just as I get to him, Rocks fires and takes out dipshit one.

With my gun trained on dipshit two, he moves from hiding. Face to face with me, the man shows no fear.

My brothers begin moving the crates as the women start to panic. One by one, my men are passing the still caged women out of the room to Hammer. Soon, they will be moving safely away from this hellhole we have rescued them from. I don't let myself relax, though.

There is still work to be done here by moving up the floors until one of us takes out Sandoval, ending his little empire of selling drugs, weapons, and flesh.

"This is bigger than you and your team of heroes," Dipshit two says to me with a sick smile. "Kill me. You won't end this. You won't find them all."

Disgusted with his apparent twisted pleasure in the threat, I lunge at him, surprising him before he can put his hands up to defend himself.

I grab him by the throat and shove him backwards until his back is against a cement pillar before I pin him in a choke hold. Ignoring his gurgles and gasps for air, I growl. "Mark my words, asshole, since they'll be some of the last you ever hear. If it's the last fuckin' thing I do, I will shut this setup down and every single person involved in it. I'm not who you think I am."

Grabbing the front of his shirt, I shove him forward and he stumbles. Fighting against my hold, I maneuver him in front of me and start walking towards the service elevator. This way, I can approach upstairs from a different entrance point. I plan to use the piece of shit as a human shield, just as he tried to do with the helpless woman he hid behind.

"You won't take me alive," he yells, ripping himself out of my grip before lunging at Rocks and grabbing for his gun.

There is a shuffle between them as I train my gun on the Cuban scumbag. My finger tightens on the trigger the second I know I can take a shot without hitting my man.

Pop.

The sound of the weapon firing rings out as both men go deathly still. Rocks stares his attacker in the eye, unflinching and uncaring, as we all watch dipshit two fall to the ground. The blood quickly starts to pour out of him, and I breathe a sigh of relief that he took the bullet and not my brother. No matter how skilled the soldier, you can never be a hundred percent sure when taking that kind of shot, and sometimes the choice is taken out of your hands in the name of necessity. It was either take the shot or risk Sandoval's man taking control of Rock's gun and ending his life.

Tying the gravely injured man to the pillar to bleed out, we leave him behind and move to help load the last girls before moving on. I might have been ready to head upstairs a few seconds ago with my hostage, but the faster we get these girls out of here, the sooner we know we can move on. It also ensures we aren't worrying about whether or not Hammer has been able to get them transported to safety. We can't take the chance that one of the subjects Coal is engaging upstairs might make his way down here and sneak up on my men.

Once we load the last crate, I bang the back of the van for Hammer to pull off so the other two vans can switch places and be ready to pick us up.

Just as I am making my way to the stairwell entrance, Coal is exiting it with a gun pointed at Sandoval's head.

"You and your band of brothers come here for what, Ice? I should have known that a bunch of low class bikers would betray me, steal my stock, and try to take over my business." The venom in his voice rolls off my name.

"I'm not here for your fucking business; I'm here to shut you down," I respond coldly.

Shock crosses his face. "I underestimated you and your club."

"No, you misunderstood our objective." He looks at me inquisitively. Unwilling to explain myself, I end our pointless conversation with a promise. "You'll soon understand."

Hammer pulls up to us, and Coal pushes Sandoval into the van then gets in beside him. Big Jim climbs up and immediately starts to restrain our captive with zip ties under Coal's watchful eyes. Hammer rounds the van, letting Skid take over driving that vehicle, while I hop in the front passenger seat, leaving Hammer to do clean up in the hotel. Rocks left with his team in the other van after loading the last girls. Hammer and his team will finish up and meet us later.

We take off and round the corner of the parking garage. As we do, a black sedan roars past us, entering the facility. I yell out Hammer's name into our comm. link, trying to warn him of the incoming threat.

Tires squeal.

Sandoval laughs.

The feed in my ear piece crackles.

"I'm down," Hammer's voice croaks through the line.

Morgan

Brooke and I spend the day around the house. I called in to work and used my last personal day. Not working sucks, but honestly, with Madyson missing, there is no way I can do my job well anyway.

Later in the day, my phone rings, the screen displaying *Blocked Caller.* Hmm … maybe it is for Madyson?

"Hello," I answer timidly.

"Morgan Powell?"

"Yes."

"This is Screech. Ice wants you to meet him at Coal's house. I'll be sending you the address."

"How do I know this is really from him?" My chest tightens as my anxiety rises. How do I know these instructions are really from Ice? What if this is some kind of lure from whatever mess my sister is in? Ice is the only person I would trust with this kind of order, and he's not the one on the other end of the line.

"There is no time to explain, just be at the address I'm sending you as fast as you can," the man replies in a rushed, brusque tone.

When the call disconnects, rather than wonder who he is and whether this is real, I dial Ice.

"No time for fuckin' explanations. Get your ass to Coal's place."

Call ended. No hello, no goodbye. The asshole is securely back in place. What is going on?

My emotions are all over the place as I quickly get ready to leave. As the text comes through with the address, I'm in the living room ready to go, and Brooke comes around the corner from the kitchen.

"Where are you going? Are you coming back here?"

"I have to go to Coal's house," I answer as I speed walk towards the front door.

"Wait!" she calls out. "I know Coal. He's my dad's Vice Prez. Can I come with you?"

"Sweetie, I don't know if it's safe or what this is about. I promise to call you, okay?" If I knew what had Ice so on edge, I would know better whether it is safe for Brooke to come. However, having so much up in the air and unknown, I don't want to put her at risk in any way.

I leave the house quickly, not giving Brooke the chance to argue. Jumping in my car, I race to the unknown address, praying this is good news instead of more bad. I don't think I can handle any more bad news.

I grip the steering wheel tightly in my hands, my knuckles turning white as my mind goes in circles. My nerves are frayed, and I am barely hanging on. If it were not for Ice helping me these past few days, I think I would have completely lost my mind by now.

Pulling up to the address, I am unprepared to find Ice pacing out front of a nondescript gray home with black shutters in a quiet, middle-class neighborhood. There is almost a dreary aura to the house that sends a chill of foreboding up my spine.

Before I can think further of how the house borders on depressing, he is at my car door, yanking it open before I can get myself unbuckled. Seeing the look on his face, I start to prepare for the worst. As soon as I am out of the car, I am in his arms, shaking, scared out of my mind.

"My sister," I whisper as my fear escalates.

"She's inside. She's alive, but they drugged her. Doc is waiting on you to examine her. I gotta go. Coal and the boys will keep you safe; they're on a rotation. I have to get to the hospital. I'll see you around." He pulls away.

"Hospital?" I question as my mind tries to absorb everything happening around me.

"Hammer was hit by a car. I gotta check on him. Then I have work to do. Go inside and be there for your sister. She's gonna need you. Brooke can come see her after she's detoxed. Coal will be in and out, but let him be. If you need anything, ask one of the other guys. They'll get it for you."

Before I get another word out, he kisses me briefly then takes off to his motorcycle. Once again, I am left wondering… what the hell happened?

Chapter
17

Morgan

Entering the house, I ignore everything about my surroundings as I race to the first bedroom where I can hear screams coming from. I stop dead in my tracks when I reach the doorway, shocked still at the sight. My heart feels like it drops to my feet and my stomach rolls. Nothing could have prepared me to find my baby sister thrashing around in a bed so wildly that she has to be restrained by the woman at her side. My gaze is frozen on my, obviously suffering, little sister as something inside of me breaks.

"It hurts so bad. Make the hurt go away," she cries out.

"Are you Morgan?" the petite woman holding my sister asks.

"Yes. Do we need to take her to the hospital?" I ask, feeling inadequate to tackle this. How in the hell do I help Madyson through this?

"Sure, if you're ready to answer a bunch of questions you don't really have answers to."

I come out of my shock at her tone. "Who are you?"

"Dr. Constance Thompson, personal physician for the Regulators Motorcycle Club." She extends her hand in greeting.

"Dr. Thompson—"

"Connie, just call me Connie or Doc," she cuts in as she cautiously backs away from the bed, since Madyson seems to have temporarily calmed down.

"What can you tell me?" I whisper, not wanting to take the chance that my sister may be able to hear or understand what we're talking about.

"I didn't want to exam her until you were present, since she does have family. She is going through the withdrawals of a cocktail they were drugging the girls with. I think heroine is involved, but I'm not sure what else they used. I need to give her a sedative then restrain her, for her safety and my own, to exam her."

I nod my head then make my way over to Madyson's side. Reaching out, I touch her hand, and she immediately recoils at my touch.

"Madyson, sweetie, it's me, Morgan."

"It hurts. Please, I'll do anything to make the pain stop. Anything!" she pleads, reaching up to clutch my shirt with her hands. My heart crumbles into a million pieces.

"Does she know where she is or what happened?" I ask the doctor, scared out of my mind.

"Most of the women that were recovered with your sister seem to be suffering some sort of memory loss. It's hard to tell. We will do a soft detox where she is given medication to wean her off slowly."

The doctor comes over, and together, we tie Madyson's arms to the bed with soft wraps. Doc administers the sedative, and we both wait to see what happens. Once Madyson relaxes into whatever oblivion she has gone into, Doc Thompson begins her exam.

While she draws tube after tube of blood, she explains it is to test for whatever chemicals are running through Madyson's system as well as any diseases she may have contracted. When she packs the tubes of blood away into her bag, she then opens her kit and removes a sterile speculum from it. I cringe, knowing what is about to happen and dreading that my sister has to endure this, even unconscious. I have had my annual physical at the gynecologist, and virgin or not, the device is not comfortable.

Turning my head away, I refuse to watch as she continues her exam of my sister's girlie parts. I hate that we have to test Madyson like this while she is out of it. It seems wrong somehow, though I also realize it is necessary.

My need to help along with my need to know causes me to finally ask, "Was s-she ..." I stammer over my words before I can continue. "Was she violated?"

"Vaginal scarring and tissue abrasions in the anal area as well lead me to believe that, yes, indeed she was. Also, her hymen is no longer intact if she was a virgin."

In my haze, I only hear snippets after that. The doctor explains the withdrawal symptoms Madyson will likely have. Abdominal and body pain. My mind scoffs, *Of course she will have pain in her body. She was raped.* Nausea. Something about keeping the trashcan handy in case she gets sick. *I would get sick to my stomach, too, if I was raped.* Sweating, chills, anxiety, paranoia, insomnia, weakness, and irritability. Is the doctor really talking withdrawal symptoms here? These all sound like things I would expect if I knew I had been raped.

She continues talking, now about the course of treatment that is needed as I zone out almost completely. I am vaguely aware that a tear is sliding down my face, but in a way, I don't really feel it. Moving to the edge of the bed, I sit down numbly while Doc Thompson dresses Madyson and reapplies the restraints.

My sister was raped.

My sister was drugged.

My sister was raped.

The ugly marks on her body make the abuse she endured evident and tell a heartbreaking story in their own silent way.

My sister was beaten.

The large, ugly, black and purple blemishes on the insides of her thighs that resemble hand marks speak of horrible, violent acts she may never recover from.

My sister was raped.

It plays on repeat in my head as I feel myself start to shut down entirely.

"Hey, hey!" a commanding voice says sharply as fingers snap right in front of my face. "I know this is a lot to process. She needs you, though. You have to pull yourself together and be strong for her."

Thoughts swirl inside my head like crazy. "Will she remember it?" I whisper while inside I beg, plead, and pray, if there is any mercy in this world, that she won't have any recollection whatsoever of the nightmare she has endured.

"Whether she does or doesn't remember, there are some great support groups and counseling available to her."

Counseling. We could all use some of that.

"Madyson, I'm so sorry. I'm here for you. I'm not going anywhere," I say softly to my sister as I lie down next to her while the doctor packs up.

Now, more than ever, I am determined to be the support system she needs. There is no way I will fail her as I have done in the past. She has become everything to me, and I will do whatever it takes to show her she does not have to walk the path ahead of her alone.

I hear the doctor leave the room, shutting the door behind her; however, I don't take my eyes off the battered and broken girl in front of me.

Seeing her like this, after days of worrying where she was and what was happening to her, is a dream come true turned into a nightmare. I would give anything, including my own life, to spare my sister what she has endured.

Now I am going to dedicate my life to being whatever it is she needs.

Ice

Getting to the hospital doesn't come fast enough as we had lose ends to tie up from this whole ordeal.

Coal has tucked away Sandoval and two of his associates we extracted alive at a secure location in three of the very same cages they had held their captives in. We will interrogate them later. For now, though, they are off the streets. Priority one is to follow up on Hammer's condition.

After his distress call, we phoned nine-one-one which brought in all the shields to swarm the area. Coal and Skid took off with Sandoval so we could keep our cover that he wasn't there.

Hammer was airlifted to a trauma hospital on the other side of the city. Knowing the driver is a low ranking man, we kept him contained for the cops. Even on Sandoval's payroll, he won't get off. Our connections run deeper than his boss's pockets. In prison, he will get shanked after he spends a few months suffering for his crimes.

With the dead bodies littering the building, of course the police had a few questions. Did we have the necessary permits to carry concealed weapons? Myself and each of my men there all showed them our permits as an answer. Why were we on private property? As they eyed us warily, hands on their holstered guns, ready to pull them on us if need be, I made one quick phone call to our man up top to explain our situation.

Less than five minutes after I hung up, the lead officer's radio squawked, informing him he needed to call his on duty Watch Commander. I watched as the man, looking confused, stepped away from us and dialed his phone. He spoke into it, listened, and then said something else back, looking very frustrated. Then all of the color drained from his face.

Hanging up the phone, he ordered the other officers to leave us alone and to start processing the crime scene. He then informed us we were free to leave.

While we were dealing with the boys in blue, I had Coal distribute the girls to Crissy's safe house then take Madyson to his own home. We are unsure of the extent of what she has endured; however, I want Morgan to feel comfortable as she helps Madyson heal.

Now, I am sitting with my brothers in the waiting room of the hospital, standing by for an update on Hammer. Pacing back and forth isn't expediting the process any, but I can't be still. Evan, Hammer's brother, came as soon as we called and actually arrived before we did.

The first time the nurse comes out, about an hour and a half after we arrived, it is to ask if there is family here for Ethan McCoy. Once Evan tells them he is Ethan's brother, she updates him with Hammer's prognosis. He is covered in superficial lacerations and bruises. From the x-rays they took, it appears as though Hammer has an intertrochanteric fracture. She goes on to explain that the fracture is between the neck of the femur and a lower bony prominence called the lesser trochanter. When the nurse sees our confused faces, she quickly adds that this means they need to take Hammer into surgery.

Time seems to stall, an endless monotony of waiting. We are all on edge, and the clock and silence seem to mock us. Six hours go by before a different nurse finally comes out.

"Family of Ethan McCoy?"

"Here." Evan jumps up and practically runs to her.

"Your brother is out of surgery. The doctor went in and inserted a nail and screw to stabilize the areas. Until he is out of recovery, we won't know the extent of nerve damage and if it will be permanent or not. The nerves in his feet are, at the moment, unresponsive to touch. As he has suffered major trauma, we were in a situation to fix what was visibly damaged, and now we'll have to wait to see what happens. I'm sorry I don't have better news right at this time."

Evan runs a shaking hand through his hair. "When can we see him?"

"Once he's out of recovery, you can see him two at a time for short periods. Please understand, his body needs rest to heal properly."

Helplessly, we pace around some more until we are finally told two of us can head back to Room 308. Evan waves for me to follow him, so I do.

As we walk down the hall, my hands get clammy. It takes everything I have not to wipe them on my pants, letting anyone who may be watching me know how jittery I am right now. I haven't felt this nervous since I went on my first Special Forces mission, unsure of what to expect.

As we open the door and walk into the room, my stomach drops.

Hammer lies on his hospital bed, eyes closed, almost as if he is sleeping peacefully. Bruises and bandages all over his body tell a different story, though.

Evan walks over to the bed and lifts the side of Hammer's blanket then gown up to expose the large bandage that covers his hip. Gently placing the gown and blanket back down, Evan then collapses in the chair next to the bed and breathes out a long sigh. He doesn't say a word, but he doesn't need to. We both know it could have been worse, which is saying something since there is no way to know if Hammer will ever walk again.

The thought of this man, my brother in both battle and on the road, never riding his bike or walking into our club again kills something inside of me. A proud man like him might not survive with his legs taken from him. The both of us have gone to more than one funeral of a soldier we have known who had lost their legs someway, somehow, in the war. They had either died of a complication of their paralysis or had taken their own life rather than live without their legs.

I can't imagine a world without a smartass, ball-busting Hammer riding on the road with me.

My mind flashes back to the last mission we were on together as Green Berets. We were in the middle of a nasty fire fight in the Kandahar Mountains against a group of terrorists we had been sent in to take out because they had taken over one of the villages in their attempt to get closer to a nearby FOB, or Forward Operating Base. We had intel saying the group had a number of high value targets that the powers that be wanted taken out.

As we marched through the rugged terrain of those mountains, making our way to the village's location, we were spotted by a couple of local goat herders. They ran ahead and warned the very men we were after of our impending arrival, causing us to basically walk into a trap.

Taking cover behind a crude mud-brick wall, I returned fire with Hammer by my side while the rest of our team moved to different vantage points around the village. We were outnumbered, taking heavy fire, and I wasn't sure if I was going to make it home to my little girl and mother.

Shit had looked pretty dire at the time, and as I ran out of ammo, I sat behind that wall, scrambling to change out for a fresh magazine. Being preoccupied with what I was doing, I didn't see one of our targets sneaking up on our flank on the opposite side of the wall.

But Hammer did.

The man ended up saving my life by putting a bullet hole in the center of that motherfucker's head. When I looked over to him, just after our enemy's body disappeared from sight, he said something that resonated through me and gained my undying loyalty.

"Don't look so fucking surprised. I'll always have your back, Ice."

Now it looks like I am going to have to figure out the best way to have Hammer's back. It is the least I can do for the man who saved my life. The man who has had my back since the moment he first joined my team in the Army. The man who has followed me from one band of brothers to another.

A man who is an integral part of what I call my family.

ICE

Chapter

18

Ice

Coal's fist strikes out, smashing into Sandoval's cheek, whipping his head to the side. While a small spray of spittle and blood flies to the already stained cement floor, he grunts, which is nothing compared to the screams he let loose earlier. I am not worried about anyone hearing us, though. We are in the soundproof basement of a house we own on the edge of Miami.

What the fucker tied hand and foot to the chair does not know is that Coal's fists and what we have already done to him are the least of his concerns. I plan on things getting a lot bloodier before we are through with him.

Since we have already choked him half to death with a garrote and ripped his fingernails off with pliers, I am sure Lazaro Sandoval thinks he can survive anything we do to him without giving us the information we want. If that is what he thinks, he is wrong.

I learned a lot of things on my missions, and how to be a sadistic, lethal motherfucker was one of them.

"Who are you? FBI? ATF? DEA?" Sandoval asks through crimson stained, swollen lips, shaking off the blow delivered by Coal as he continues to spit blood with every word he speaks.

"I'm your worst fuckin' nightmare, that's who I am," I answer in a merciless voice.

"People will look for me. The police will look for me, even. I have quite a few of them on my payroll. Do you honestly think they will want to lose the money they make from me? They will find out what you've done and come for me." There is trepidation in his voice. I can tell what he says and what he worries will actually happen are two different things. Good. He should be scared shitless, because I don't plan to let him out of this basement alive.

We have spent hours torturing him meticulously. Finally, he is starting to break. He is crumbling like any man—no matter how strong willed they are—would after the things we have done. There is more to come, though. Before we are finished here, he will give me everything I want.

"Clue in, Sandoval. We override anything the cops want to do. I have a clearance that rivals the Vice President's. There are very few people in this country that have power over me. Doesn't matter if I slit your throat in front of the chief of police, not one of them could touch me."

His eyes go wide in surprise as the realization of his predicament dawns on him.

"That's right, fucker; we aren't your regular motorcycle gang. I'm a Harley ridin' deliverer of death. I could pick up the phone right now, call the President of the United States, and tell him that I'm going to cut you into tiny pieces and spread them over the ocean for the fish to eat. And he would tell me to go right on ahead."

Little does Sandoval know that scenario is not too far off from what I will be doing to him.

"You tell me where the other girls are stashed, and I'll introduce you to the hell you're heading to quickly. The longer you take, the longer I'll take. Either way, today is the day you die."

Our captive does his best to straighten his back, and what little pride he thinks he has left shines through his eyes as he answers me. "If you plan to kill me, why should I tell you anything I know? Perhaps I shall take my secrets to the grave."

He won't be taking anything to his proverbial grave except that black soul of his. Although, I have to admit, I once again see why he was able to build his small empire. Here he is, bruised, bleeding, and death invariably breathing down his neck, yet he sits there with the sort of proud presence of a king instead of the defeated scumbag he really is.

Time to change that.

"Coal, hand me the blow torch and set this asshole on his back. Let's see how long he can last before he starts crying like the little bitch he really is."

My VP hands me my torch, and I let Sandoval see it before Coal tips his chair back and lets him harshly fall to the floor. A small shout of pain escapes him as his head cracks open on the unforgiving surface, giving him yet another wound from which he starts to bleed.

As I turn on the blow torch, he raises his head and looks at me defiantly. I let a ruthless smile spread across my face while I watch sweat beading on his forehead. He is about to do a fuck of a lot more than sweating.

Bringing the blow torch down, I hold it under the soles of his dress shoes and watch as the bottoms start to burn and melt away. Sandoval begins to struggle against his bindings as he feels the heat, although we both know he is not going anywhere. The flame disintegrates the bottom of his shoe in seconds, and then the man who raped and tortured numerous women, making them scream in pain, is the one who is screaming.

I start at the top of his foot and move my way to his heel, ignoring the smell of burnt rubber, leather, and human flesh. Moving over to his other foot, I repeat the process. His voice is already hoarse from his pained howls, and by the time Coal and I are done, his vocal cords will probably be ruined and bleeding.

He deserves every second of this agony. I have no qualms about dishing out his punishment.

When Sandoval passes out from the pain, I pull the blowtorch away from his foot. Turning it off, I tell Coal to sit him back up. Once he does, I give my man his next directive.

"Slap that little bitch back to consciousness."

Coal's lips tip up on one side in a vicious sneer.

The first slap makes Sandoval shake his head incoherently. The second slap has him crying out yet doesn't bring him fully around. Instead, he is in a state of semi-consciousness. The third slap finally brings him back to awareness, and the once proud man is now sobbing in pain.

"Where are the women?"

He doesn't answer me, only continues to cry.

I motion for Coal to grab the large bucket of cold water we had ready against the wall, and I point at our prisoner. When the water hits Sandoval in the face, he sputters and shakes his head in shock.

Looking up at me, he sees the fiery weapon I kept in my hand and begins to shake from head to toe. His gaze travels upwards to lock on to my own determined eyes, and a new wet spot starts to spread across the crotch of his pants, a small stream falling to the floor.

He has every reason to piss himself. I plan to ruin him like he ruined the countless women who have crossed his path.

"Where are the women, Sandoval?"

His breath starts to saw in and out of his chest in small, panicked puffs of air. However, he shakes his head again, refusing to say a word.

"You give me an answer, or I turn this blowtorch back on. Only, this time, I won't stop at your feet. I'll burn my way up your legs, over that small excuse you call a dick, and I won't stop until I get to your eyeballs. So, I suggest you start talking before I start barbequing your ass alive."

I know the look on my face conveys exactly how serious I am about carrying out the deadly promise, and he must realize it, too, because he hangs his head in defeat.

"Many of them are gone or dead, sold off to other powerful men overseas: foreign politicians, sheiks, and crime lords throughout Europe and the Asian countries," he blubbers.

A red haze covers my vision at the thought of all the women I now know I might not be able to track down and save.

"Did you keep any kind of records?" I bark at him, angry that I don't have the time to spend torturing him, keeping him on the brink of life, before I finally give him death.

His head bobs up and down frantically. "In my safe at the hotel. If I give you the combination, you will let me leave here with my life. I will disappear back to Cuba, and you shall never lay eyes on my face again." He thinks he now has a bargaining chip to save himself.

He is wrong. I do not negotiate with the sort of scum I will be scraping off the soles of my boots later.

Without taking my eyes off of my captive's, I answer him ominously, "Did you know that my man here is part Sioux? He may not look it beyond his tan, but his grandfather came straight off the reservation. Want to know one of the things his grandfather taught him? Here, let me have him show you. It's this old timer practice from back before the English colonized here … called scalping. Show him how it's done, Coal."

Sandoval starts thrashing in his chair so hard he tips himself over and falls on his side. Even after the *oomph* of his fall, he does not stop his wiggling, desperately trying to get away from my brother as he unsheathes his large hunting knife from his thigh.

When Sandoval sees Coal bending over, his hand reaching for his hair, he once again starts screaming bloody murder.

The man does not have a chance in hell of escaping his fate.

Coal grabs Sandoval's thick, black hair in a tight grip and places his knife against the upper part of our detainee's forehead. Slowly, as to drag out the misery of what is about to happen, Coal makes an incision. Then he drags the knife to the back of Sandoval's neck and around again to his original incision at the man's forehead, taking his slow, sweet time while our victim screams hoarsely in agony. Finally, my brother puts his foot on one shoulder, bracing his calf on the back of the chair, and pulls the Cuban Don's hair off with both hands, from front to back.

By the time Coal is done, Sandoval's voice is almost gone, and he is weeping uncontrollably. My VP tosses the bloody scalp on the floor and then tips the chair back up to sit on its legs. Rivers of red run down Sandoval's face, dripping on his pants legs as his head hangs down until his chin is touching his chest.

"Give me the combination to your safe, and then give me the location of any women you still have hidden away. You do that, and your pain ends."

A silent moment passes before Sandoval's defeated voice finally croaks, "Thirteen, twenty-three, ninety-six."

"And the women?"

"Bahamas. Andros Island. I own a large compound on the south part of the island."

"Anything else you want to tell me?" I ask, done with the man in front of me and anxious to leave to check on Brooke and Madyson.

"If you let me free, I will give you every cent in my bank account," he feebly pleads.

A booming laugh escapes me, making him flinch. "One of my men has already seized your accounts, all six of them, you sly bastard. You're already penniless."

Standing up, I look one last time at the man who used to be known as the Cuban Terror. He is now a shell of a man who knows his last breath is near. "Cut him up into pieces, and then call Dwayne over at the Everglades. Go out with him on the airboat to Gator Island and feed this prick to the 'gators. I'm goin' to call Lucas, let him know we got justice for his two men that died because of this fucker. They also have to get their shit together now. The Ex Ops Team is going to have to track down and rescue any of the women that can be found from the records in the safe. Overseas is beyond our territory, capabilities and pay grade."

Giving Coal a chin lift, I pull out my cell phone, preparing to dial Lucas's number. "Let me know when you're done getting rid of the trash."

As I turn and walk away, Lazaro Sandoval asks me what will be his last question. "Will you kill me first?" At my continued silence he begs. "Please!"

Turning my head to look at him, I note his bleak look of acceptance as I ask back, "Did you spare any of the women you kidnapped any pain?"

His head drops to his chest again.

"That's what I thought. Coal there is going to give you as much mercy as you gave those woman—*none*."

With that promise, I leave my brother to finish the job, satisfied that justice has been served and Sandoval will soon be taking his final breath.

The screams start before I close the door behind me.

ICE

Chapter
19

Morgan

Three Weeks Later...

"You need anything before I head out?" Coal asks from the doorway of what is temporarily my sister's room. He has been a rock solid support for us.

I have stayed here with Madyson through the slow detox process: the vomiting, the chills, the sweats, the pain, and the nightmares she can't remember when she wakes. Through everything she has endured, I have remained steadfast at her side.

Ice hasn't been around much. He has called here and there, but I haven't seen him. For a few days after we arrived here, Coal didn't come home at all. Now we have found a routine in being here. Coal checks in, and we have formed our own friendship. He never comes close to Madyson, though; never comes inside the room, only stands in the doorway.

"No, Coal. Thank you for everything," I reply as he looks over at Madyson's peacefully sleeping figure.

"How is she?"

"The withdrawals have passed. The meds seemed to ease it. She is coming off those now. She doesn't remember anything of her actual captivity. Her last memory before waking up here was being asked by a man to hold a cable on his car so he could get it started. Everything after that is a blur. At least, that is what she tells me. Sometimes I wonder if she remembers more than that and just doesn't want to tell me. I see the battle in her eyes as she fights to push back the darkness that is ruling her life. She gets upset because she feels like she should've known better. She was having cramps and wanted relief. Instead, she got a lifetime of scars."

Something dark passes through Coal's features. "Make sure she gets whatever help she needs. Don't let this haunt her." Without another word, he turns and leaves me standing there, wondering what ghosts are chasing him.

My morning passes as every morning has lately. I make breakfast, try to help Madyson get through her school work, clean up, and go through the motions of refusing to allow myself to breakdown as my sister struggles. The reality is daunting. She can't concentrate. I don't blame her, but we need to make some decisions. She has missed too many days, and the school wants answers. I don't have them to give, and Madyson doesn't want to talk about it. She tells me constantly that she doesn't want to think about her future.

When my phone vibrates in my back pocket, the screen flashes the name *Ice*, and my heart flutters a little in my chest.

"Hello," I greet, trying to be cheerful. I don't want to be a concern or burden for him.

"How ya doin'?" Ice asks, much in the same way he does every time he checks in. He may not be here physically; however, he calls and texts enough to make it known we are on his mind.

"Getting by. Coal has been great," I reply honestly.

"He has, has he?" Ice says sarcastically.

Surely, he is not jealous of Coal? I haven't seen Ice in weeks, and he wants to be a smartass on the phone with me?

"Considering my sister and I have all but moved into his house without warning or a real invitation, yeah, I would say he's been great."

"You could move in with Brooke and me anytime you want. We put you there to begin with so your sister could have her privacy until she was ready to see Brooke. Since my daughter has been there every day, since two days after her rescue, I would say my house would be the best place for you."

"Where do you come up with this stuff?" I question harshly. This man is exasperating. "Why would I think we were welcome to stay there?"

"Why wouldn't you be? Clue in, woman. It was my bed you were sleepin' in before you went there, and it'll be my bed you're sleepin' in when it's all said and done."

"Where I slept is irrelevant. This entire thing has been a crazy, adrenaline fueled matter of circumstance, and when Madyson is ready to go home, we're going back to my place," I say, unable to comprehend exactly what he is telling me.

Is he serious? I don't want to get my hopes up and then be let down. Do I want to share a bed with Brett 'Ice' Grady? The answer is yes, I do. However, we come from two completely different worlds. That does not mean I cannot see past his gruff biker exterior. Because I do. There is a softer side to this man. There is this loyalty that drives him to take care of those he calls his own. Seeing him with his daughter is pure, unconditional love at its finest. There is infinitely more to this man than the asshole I first met. That doesn't mean the two of us together makes sense.

He is the kind of man who does whatever he wants without asking for permission. He reminds me of that phrase, *'It's better to ask forgiveness than to ask for permission.'*

I have always lived by other people's opinions and rules, never stepping out of those carefully drawn lines people, like my parents, laid down for me. I am the kind of woman who waits for the green light before crossing the street because I don't want to get a ticket for jaywalking. His world consists of people who do not walk on the right side of the law. I am not stupid; it didn't take me long to realize he and his men have not only stepped over to the criminal side, in some aspects, they run it in this area. I am simply not certain to what extent their business goes.

How can this possibly work between us?

"Kissin' me was a crazy, adrenaline fueled matter of circumstance, huh? You didn't even know where I was goin' or what I was doin', so you can't say that kiss was for good luck or because you were afraid it would be goodbye. So then, tell me, sweetheart, what was that all about?"

Oh, my goodness, he is actually going to talk about it. The best kiss I have ever had. The kiss I can't get out of my mind. The kiss I want to replay over and over again so perhaps I can feel a phantom caress of his lips across my own. The kiss I want to happen again, as well as so much more, and he actually wants to talk about it? No! This is mortifying.

"It was a crazy … ummm … moment of weakness," I stammer out.

"Sweetheart, I'd be more than happy to make you weak, just not in the way you're referring to. But I'm warnin' you now, don't give me some line of bullshit that you aren't cravin' another kiss from me. I bet you enjoyed my mouth on you so much that, if I had stuck my hand down your pants, your cream would have coated my fingers."

What a cocky bastard! I am completely embarrassed. I have never talked about a kiss after it happened. Not that I have that many kisses under my belt. Nor have I ever been spoken to in such a way about something as intimate as a body's physical reaction. Is this what it is supposed to be like? God, when I finally have sex, does that require a discussion, too?

I hear a feminine voice call his name in the background, giving me the perfect escape. A curl of jealousy moves through me, but I push it aside. It is probably one of the strippers at After Midnight, and even if it wasn't, I have no claim over the man who consumes more of my thoughts than he should. He could boink half of Florida, and I would have no right to say anything to him about it.

"You're busy. I'll let you go," I rush out, eager to get him off the phone so I can try to straighten my head out about this man who haunts me in too many ways.

"There's no letting go between us, Morgan. Get that straight right now. I'm man enough to see something I want and not be afraid to go for it. I do have to handle business, though. I'll be in touch." The call is disconnected without another word, and I am left feeling like I am very much in over my head with this man.

The day passes with Ice remaining on my mind. After Madyson passes out from exhaustion, I am sitting in Coal's living room, watching the television, when I hear the front door open and close. Thinking it is Coal coming home, I don't bother to turn around. Although he has been nothing except nice, I try to stay out of his way to avoid bothering him.

I hear the heavy thunk of booted steps on the floor behind me and assume Coal is walking towards the back of the house to where his bedroom is located. Sometimes, he comes home long enough to shower and change before heading out to wherever it is he goes to give us space. However, when the footsteps stop directly behind me on the other side of the couch I freeze, my body tensing.

Leaning my head backwards, I look up to see Ice staring back down at me. The expression on his face has my heart immediately pounding in my chest. No man has ever looked at me like this, like he wants to consume me, eat me alive. The thought makes me blush.

The side of his mouth kicks up and he murmurs, "I'd pay a pretty penny to know what the thought is that made your face flush like that."

The fact that he notices my blush only makes it worse.

"What are you doing here?" I whisper.

"Came to see if we could have another adrenaline fueled matter of circumstance."

It is official. I am positive that I am now red from embarrassment from the top of my head to the tips of my toes.

"If I were to peel your clothes of right now, would I see that gorgeous pink color all over?"

Like I am going to answer that. "I thought you had business to attend to?"

"Got the business for the day done, babe."

"Including the woman who called your name when we were on the phone?" My mouth snaps shut as soon as the question leaves my mouth. Why in the world did I ask that? I could have sworn I had gotten it through my head that it was none of my business what Ice does.

I watch as his eyebrow cocks up. Then he looks at me as if I am a puzzle. Right when I am about to tell him to forget what I have said, he moves around the couch and comes to stand in front of me. Turning, he pushes back the wooden coffee table a little bit and then sits down on it, facing me. His elbows are on his thighs, his hands hanging between his legs, and his face is an impervious mask I cannot read.

"For a woman who told me we were nothing but an adrenaline fueled excuse earlier, that comment sounded awfully jealous. You wanna explain that to me?"

Unsure what to say, I shake my head.

"Okay, then I'm gonna explain shit to you. You're mine." He holds up his hand when I open my mouth to protest. "Nope, keep your mouth shut till I'm done talkin'. Like I said, you're mine. I gave you some time to help get your sister settled, and now I'm done wastin' it. I want you. I'm gonna have you, and you're damn well gonna have me in every way that counts. You understand what I'm sayin' to you?"

Oh, my God. Did he just insinuate what I think he did?

"Yeah, babe, I did. And, in case you didn't know it, you said that out loud. Now, let me explain to you what else that comment meant. I don't do the jealousy bullshit. While we are whatever we are, you're not gonna come at me verbally swingin' some bullshit about other women. I work with 'em. I don't touch 'em. Get over it."

Anger and uncertainty fill me. "You expect me to believe you're going to be faithful to me when I've heard about the revolving door on your bedroom?"

"There is no revolving door on my bedroom. That implies I bring women to my home to fuck 'em, and that's something I rarely do because of Brooke. I usually fuck 'em at the club. The few that have come to the house are when I know she won't be home and they never stay."

My mouth drops open in surprise at his frank comments about his sex life. "And, after that comment, do you really believe I'll think you would be faithful to me?"

Ice leans forward, reaches his hand out, snags me by the back of my neck, and pulls me forward so we are nose to nose. We are breathing the same air, filling all of my senses with him.

In a low, husky voice, he then says, "Yeah, Morgan, I do. If I have to fuck you three times a day to prove that I'm not takin' my dick anywhere else, I will. Believe me when I say, I don't want any other woman but you. Don't ask me why, because I can't explain it. All I know is that you make me think things I haven't thought about since Brooke's mom died. You make me feel things I thought had died inside of me long ago. Now that you woke me up, babe, you're gonna live life with me. I figure I can teach you how to pull that stick out of your ass to live wild and free. In return, you can teach me how to go from day to day havin' someone in my life that I care about like this without worryin' they're gonna leave me again."

My breath rushes out, deflating me and my anger into nothing. How can a man this strong be afraid of anything?

"Why would I need to teach you that, Ice?"

He runs his nose along the ridge of my own. "Lost my wife, baby. That does somethin' to a man. It makes him want to close off the part of himself that lets anyone in, the part that feels too much when someone he cares about disappears. Besides Brooke and my brothers, I had done exactly that. Then you came into my life, flashin' your cute and makin' me want more. Now I've decided you're gonna give it to me. Thing is, I promise you'll like given' it to me."

I nibble on my bottom lip. "Maybe I'm scared to give into you."

He smiles. "Guess I'm gonna have to convince you then, baby." He doesn't give me a chance to respond. His lips crash down on mine in a hungry urgency that makes my toes curl. I feel his tongue do a searching sweep across the seam of my own lips, and I open myself to his invasion. There is something about this man that is hard to say no to. Besides, if I am honest with myself, I don't want to tell him no. Every fiber of my being wants to tell him yes to everything, especially when he kisses me like this.

Our tongues tangle, his sweet, minty taste making me moan. It is intoxicating, heady. We kiss for who knows how long, until I become lightheaded. I would happily pass out into oblivion as long as Ice's firm lips never left my own. He finally pulls back from our intoxicating kiss and rests his forehead against my own while we pant, trying to catch our breath.

"Damn you taste sweet. Wish I could stay and taste you more, but I need to get home to Brooke."

My mind is in a haze of dazed pleasure, making me addle-brained and unable to respond; therefore, I simply nod my head.

Pulling back, he gives me a kiss on my forehead before standing up and stepping away. Just as he moves to take another step, he places a plastic grocery bag on the table in front of me.

"What's this?"

He gives me a wicked grin. "Thought I'd bring you something sweet to eat since I plan to be eating something sweet soon." He laughs at the appalled look on my face. Then, giving me a mischievous wink, he walks out of the house, leaving me to my bewildered thoughts.

How is it that this man always manages to leave me speechless and unsure of what he will say or do next? I am not sure if I will ever be able to handle all that encompasses the man known as Ice.

ICE

Chapter
20

Ice

One Week Later...

"Did you know Morgan may have to call her parents and move home with Madyson?" Brooke asks me as she finishes getting ready for us to meet the very women she just mentioned.

We are supposed to be helping them pack up from Coal's and get them back to Morgan's place. They don't really have a lot of stuff, but the girls want to hang out, and I want to see Morgan again. This week kept me busy with club business; as a result, I haven't seen her since I dropped off that dessert I bought her. What my daughter is telling me now, though, makes me think I should have asked my woman more questions when she sounded so distracted on the phone.

"What the fuck are you talkin' about?"

"Morgan missed too much time at work. They replaced her. She's been applying for jobs, but hasn't found anything. She doesn't have much left in her savings account, and Madyson isn't ready to work. She already dropped out of school for this year. They don't have anywhere to go but back home. At least, until

Morgan can get a job. And that is if their parents will even let them come back."

"Stay here. I'll be back," I order, walking out the door and straight to my bike.

Waiting is not my strong suit. For her, I will wait; for this, I will not.

In my impatience, I make a call to my in-house tech geek for her location. Screech lets me know she seems to be en route to her condo.

Yes, I am still tracking her phone. I have no intention of stopping, either.

Pulling up to her place, I don't see her car in the parking lot, but I know she can't be far behind me. That's okay; I have something I want to take care of before she gets here anyway.

After I accomplish my short mission, I head back to my bike, leaning against it until I see Morgan's little car pull in and park. I am not waiting very long when she walks up carrying a duffle bag of her belongings.

"Ice," she greets, studying me curiously. "I wasn't expecting you here. You didn't have to wait around for me. You know my number; why didn't you call?"

"I didn't want to be expected, and I didn't want to call. Where's Madyson?" I clip out.

"At Coal's, packing our toiletries and the last of the clothes," she answers uncertainly.

I can tell she is picking up on my anger and is confused as to why I am in the mood that I am in. She bites her bottom lip, and as cute as it is, it does nothing to curb the ire building in me. She is walking to her doorstep as I continue on alongside her.

She is still trying to figure me out when she hesitantly adds, "I told you not to come. We don't need more help. You all have done so much. I'll never be able to repay you for what you've done for us."

Taking the bag from her arm, I move aside for her to unlock the front door. As soon as we enter, I start the inquisition.

"Why didn't you tell me?" I ask, shutting and locking the door behind us.

"Tell you what?"

Facing her, I bark back, "Your job. Your living arrangements. Your financial situation. Why didn't you tell me?"

She takes the bag from me with no response. Making her way down the hall, she carries it to her bedroom as if she is running from me. I snort. Like I am going to let her run from me this time. My woman is about to learn some hard lessons. As in, you do not hide your problems from your man.

"It's not your problem; it's mine. You know, take responsibility and all that," she fires back. I can tell she is unnerved by the way I am dogging her heels, unwilling to let her ignore me.

She moves to her closet, only I grab her wrist and tug her to me. As she stumbles, I pull her against me tightly. Wrapping my arm around her waist, I cup her ass with my large hand and squeeze. Then, with my free hand, I cup her chin and tilt her head back to look at me.

"Sweetheart, you're playin' with fire. That mouth of yours is gonna get you in trouble."

Her eyes dance in challenge, turning me on more.

"This isn't your concern," she whispers as her breathing picks up. Yes, I am driving her as crazy as she is me.

"Everything about you is my concern."

"I promised Madyson it's only temporary until I can get a new job. We can help Mallory this way, too. Being with her we can all work together to get out again. I don't even know if my parents will let us come back; again, it's not your problem."

"No."

"What do you mean, no? Ice, this isn't for you to decide."

Damn, it makes me hard when she gets feisty. I am about to piss her off a whole lot more, too.

"Rent's paid up for the rest of the year. Took care of that when I first got here."

"I can't let you do that!" she shrieks in frustration.

"Already done."

"I still have to pay utilities and food. Madyson is having anxiety issues and needs her medication. I need to go home until I have a job again. Paying my rent doesn't fix my problems, Ice; it just puts a temporary band-aid on them."

"Fine. You work for me. You got a job, you got a place, and the rent is paid. Next problem."

She tries to pull away from me, but it only causes me to grip her tighter.

"I can't strip!" Her fear shows as she wiggles against me, still trying to get away, making my dick harder.

"Fuck no. You aren't stripping. Well, you can strip for me, but only for me, where no one else can see that sweet little body of yours. I'm talkin' about you doin' the books at the two clubs. I need an accountant to keep the shit straight, and I hate doin' it. Now I have you, problem solved. What else you got for me to solve, baby?"

"What are we doing, Ice?" she asks, licking her lips nervously.

"I'm giving you a job," I answer honestly. I had already thought of offering Morgan the job. I liked the thought of her being where I can get to her any time I want. Her situation merely gives me the excuse to do it sooner rather than later.

"You're makin' me a whore."

Stepping away from her, anger consumes me. "Is that what you really fuckin' think? I'm an ass, but I'm not a piece of shit. Tell me, Morgan, have you sucked my dick? Have you let me fuck that sweet pussy or, better yet, that tight fuckin' ass? No! So how am I makin' you a whore?"

"You're buying me off with illegal money! I'm not stupid. The Regulators do shady stuff. I know you're criminals," she stammers.

"Is that what you really think of me, woman? That all I am is a criminal? It's never occurred to you that I might be more? You really think Brooke would stay with me if I was no good?"

She doesn't speak. She doesn't move. We have a silent stand-off in her room.

Putting my hands on my hips, I try to calm my temper. "The money you would be paid with is clean. It comes from the clubs. There is nothing illegal about owning and operating strip clubs."

"There is more to the Regulators than strip clubs and Harleys. You wouldn't have found my sister if you ran two completely legitimate businesses," she firmly states, gaining her resolve.

"How quick you are to judge ... tsk, tsk, tsk ... How wrong and right you are. The Regulators are so much more than strip clubs and motorcycles. Let me ask you something. Do you trust me?"

"That's an unfair question." She crosses her arms over her chest, making her breasts stand out more.

"Have I ever lied to you? Misled you? Would I ever intentionally put you in danger? What does your gut tell you about me and my brothers? Hell, you have lived with Coal for how long now? How do you judge us so freely?" I bite out at her. "Do you trust me?" I ask her again, with vehemence this time.

"Yes," she whispers, meeting my stare.

"What I'm about to tell you can never be repeated. If it is, it could forfeit both of our lives. Understand?"

She nods back at me, yet her skeptic thoughts are written all over her face. Tough shit. She is going to listen to what I have to say, absorb that shit, and finally pull the godforsaken stick out of her ass. There is a difference in getting hard for Miss Prim and Proper and getting pissed off over her sometimes judgmental attitude.

"I'm part of a government undercover team placed here in Miami to regulate or take down anything Uncle Sam considers major illegal activities in the Southeastern United States. Sometimes that happens to be in my territory, as in the case that Madyson stumbled into, and sometimes that means I go out of state for short periods of time to handle whatever it is they need me to handle. Things aren't always what they seem; the Regulators are an example of that."

Her mouth drops open in surprise.

"I may be bad to the bone, baby, but sometimes bad people do good things. Coal is an example. His past would be one where most people would consider him bad, but has he been bad to you? Not in the least."

"What did he do?" her quivering voice asks.

"That's his story to tell, not mine." I make my way back over to her. "Good people sometimes do bad things for the greater good. That is the Regulators MC. I can't give you any more than that. Can you live with that? Can you handle being with a man who does bad things sometimes for the greater good?"

"I'm not with you, Ice."

Putting my hands on either side of her face, my lips slam down on hers, and without hesitation, she opens for me. I slip my tongue between her lips, softly gliding it over her teeth. My tongue tangles with hers while her hands come up around my neck, pulling me into her.

As her body melts into mine, I move one hand to grip the back of her neck and hold her to me. My other hand moves to cup her ass and rock her into my now rock-hard erection. When she moans and becomes more aggressive, I pull away, leaving her panting.

"Tell me again how you aren't with me," I state before capturing her mouth with my own again.

She kisses me back as fiercely as I am ravaging her mouth, and wild abandon takes over. My hands go down to her thighs, gripping them in an unforgiving hold. Effortlessly, I scoop her up, wrapping her legs around my waist as I walk us over to her bed. I lay her back then break our kiss to drop my mouth to her neck. Nipping, sucking, I refuse to hold back as I consume her, leaving my mark on her creamy skin wherever I can so the world will see my ownership of her.

She paws at my shirt, tugging it up before I pull away to finish taking it off and throw it to the side. As I lie back over her, she freezes, making me pause.

Has she changed her mind? Her body tells me one thing, though now I am afraid that mind of hers that never seems to stop going in ridiculous circles is convincing her this is a bad idea. Damn, I hope not.

"Morgan?"

"Umm … Ice—"

"No," I command her in a rough voice. "In bed, I'm Brett to you. When you call out my name, it will be my real name you scream."

Her mouth forms a little 'O' before she again is biting that bottom lip of hers, driving me nuts with the urge to lean down and do the same.

"I need to tell you something, Brett."

"You really wanna talk right now?" I ask, wondering how we went from really hot to a fucking conversation so quickly. There is an innocence that washes over her features, and it dawns on me.

She murmurs, "Umm …"

"You've never done this before," I state, watching her reaction intently.

When her nails dig into my arms as she slowly nods her head, the breath I had not realized I was holding rushes out of my body, and I drop my head to her chest. Trying to calm my body, I lie there as still as a statue. For the first time since I became a man, I am unsure how to proceed. I don't want to rush her, but Goddamn, I want her so badly I can fucking taste it.

Her hands slide up my body to my head. Running her fingers through my hair, she tugs my head up, resting her hands on either side of my face to make sure she gets my attention.

"I want this. I want this with you. I'm nervous, and you will ... umm ... have to ... ermm ... teach me," she whispers nervously. "That is, if you still want to. I've read some men are turned off by..." she begins to ramble in the cute way that is all Morgan Ann Powell.

Rocking my still hard dick against her, I state the obvious, "Sweetheart, does that feel turned off to you?"

She smiles up at me as she shakes her head in answer.

"You sure about this?" I ask, needing to know she isn't feeling pressured. "I'm not good at gentle. I'll do my best not to fuck you through the mattress, though."

Without a word, she pulls me down to kiss her.

I wasn't lying to her when I said I don't do gentle, but for her, I will do my best for as long as I can manage it.

Running my large hands down her body, I slip them under the hem of her shirt and slowly pull it up, placing kisses on each inch of skin I reveal. When I uncover her pink, lacy bra, it is hard not to come in my jeans. Her lingerie is sweet and innocent, just like her.

Now that innocence will always be mine.

I push her shirt up under her chin then hook a finger over the top of the delicate lace covering her right breast and pull it down until her nipple pops out. The little bud is dusky pink, hard, and ready for me. I lean down and nibble on it, enjoying Morgan's gasp of surprise.

Anxious to hear more of her sexy sounds, I suck the nipple into my mouth and lash my tongue over it. Her back bows up under me, and I brace myself with a hand on either side of her body.

Pulling away, I look at her glazed expression. "I wonder if you could come from my mouth on those luscious, little nipples." Pulling her shirt over her head and unsnapping her bra, I continue, "I don't have the patience to find out now, but you can bet your sweet ass I'll find out later."

I give her a fast, hard kiss before I use my tongue to lick down her neck, between her breasts, down her abdomen, and around her belly button. Then I look up her body to her face and watch her gaze at me as I unbutton and unzip her jeans before peeling them down her legs with her panties. I want her naked and bare, writhing beneath me as I cover her with my body. She is making me crazy already, and I have not even tasted her where I really want to.

Tossing her jeans on the floor, I smooth both of my hands up the soft skin of her legs, bending them as I go so her feet rest on the mattress. I then push her thighs wide so she is open to me.

At the sight of her pussy, covered in trimmed curls and already glistening for me, I feel my cock jerk in my jeans. It's almost as if that bastard has a mind of his own and is impatient to get where I can't take my eyes off of.

"Brett?" I hear her ask hesitantly.

"Yes, baby?" I answer without moving my eyes from the juncture of her thighs.

"Is it ... is everything okay?"

"Oh, hell yeah. This is the prettiest little pussy I've ever seen." I finally raise my eyes to look at her face, loving the blush spreading across her cheeks and down her neck. My shy little virgin is worried I don't like her body. It is time to prove to her exactly how much I love it.

Reaching into my back pocket, I pull out my wallet and remove the condom from inside it. It is hard not to laugh at the way Morgan's eyes go wide as she watches me throw it down on the bed next to her leg.

While she stares at the little foil packet, I unbutton and start to unzip my own jeans. She hears the rasping sound and turns her head to watch my movements. I don't want her to get scared at the size of my cock, so I shuck my jeans quickly and lie down on the bed before she can get a good look.

"I-Ice?" she stammers, propping herself on her elbows to look at me.

Taking the palm of my hand, I lightly slap over her pussy in reprimand. She gives a surprised little shriek.

"What did I tell you to call me in the bedroom, Morgan?"

"B-Brett."

"That's right, sweetheart. You remember that because I want to hear you moaning it in a few seconds, since my tongue is going to be buried between these pink little lips of yours." I run my finger around her cleft, collecting her juices and spreading them over her clit. "You ready, baby?"

Her head falls back a little bit as she moans, "Yesss."

Lowering my head, I lightly lick up her opening, pulling her syrupy taste into my mouth. Her body jerks at the contact, but I don't stop. I part her swollen folds with my tongue and then spear it inside of her, feeling her tightness for the first time. I groan at the sensation, knowing that, when I finally get inside of her, it is going to be a hot, tight, perfect fit around my cock.

Morgan starts whimpering as I swirl my tongue around her opening, inside her, and then back out to swipe over her clit. When she tries to wiggle, I clamp my hands over her hips, stopping the movements and keeping her exactly where I want her.

"Please, Brett, please. You're killing me."

"Please what, Morgan?"

"I need more!" she wails.

"You want more of my tongue, sweetheart?" I glide a finger around her opening and then stick the tip inside and wiggle it. "Or do you want my fingers?"

"Ah! Your fingers! Please, your fingers."

Using my free hand, I push back on her thigh, leaving her even more exposed to me. Then I slowly push the finger already inside of her further in, taking my time so she can feel everything I do to her in excruciating detail. When the tip of my finger bumps against her hymen, I stop, not ready to take that step yet. I want to build her higher, make her hotter, before I rip the last physical evidence of her innocence away.

Bringing my lips down on her clit, I give it a strong suck and feel Morgan buck underneath me. My finger doesn't stop moving in and out of her hot depths as I kiss and suck her clit, making her go wild.

Pulling my mouth from her, I ask to make sure, "You ready for more?"

"Yes!" she sobs in wild abandon. "I need more, Brett. God, I need more."

"Then more is what you'll get, baby."

I push two fingers inside of her. Feeling her stretch around me as I pump her slowly, yet not too deeply. I go back to loving her clit until she is squirming almost uncontrollably on the bed.

It is time to take what is mine—that barrier—and this time, I am not asking if she is ready.

When I pull my fingers out, she cries a little protest until she feels them at her entrance again. Then, once again, I cover her clit with my mouth, this time sucking harshly as I slam all three fingers as far as they will go inside of her, tearing through her barrier and claiming Morgan for good.

I keep my attention on her clit as best as I can while I pump, wiggling and stretching her with my fingers to prepare her for the part of me that is much longer.

Morgan is now moaning continuously, breathing ragged breaths, as her internal muscles start to pulse around my digits. She is on the verge of an orgasm, and I don't want her first one with me to be anywhere other than on my cock.

Pulling my fingers from her body, I grab the foil packet, rip it open with my teeth, and then roll it down my aching flesh. I then maneuver myself over her, situating myself between her legs, before moving one of my hands up until it is sliding underneath her head to fist her hair in my hand. Pulling only hard enough to give her the slightest pinch of erotic pain, I tip her head forward and force her eyes to meet mine.

"You ready to be mine, Morgan Powell?"

Breathlessly, she answers, "Yes, Brett."

"About damn time."

As I fit my cock to her entrance, she whimpers. Dropping my lips to the shell of her ear, I try to soothe her as I start to ease my tip inside. "Shhh, sweetheart. Nothing but pleasure, that's what I'm gonna give you." I slide in an inch, holding myself there, feeling her unused muscles stretch around me.

"Will it hurt, Brett?" she cries softly. "How bad will it hurt?"

"Nothing but pleasure, baby, promise. I'll always give you nothing but pleasure."

I slide in another inch, feeling my control start to fray. This slow pace won't last forever. My restraint can only last so long, although I am doing my best to make it last as long as possible for her.

Her hands grip my shoulders, her nails digging into the skin there, and the sharp pinch sends a frisson of pleasure down my spine. I jerk in response, burying another inch inside of her.

"Ah! You're stretching me. It burns."

"You burning up for me Morgan?" I whisper in her ear, slowly pulling myself out in case I am hurting her. "Good burn or bad burn, sweetheart?"

"It burns so good, Brett. Oh, God, I never knew it could burn this good."

The last of my control disintegrates with her words, and I surge forward. Her hips rise to mine, as if she is trying to get closer, burying me farther inside, but I don't think that is possible. I am in her to the hilt, holding steady one final time in a last ditch attempt to let her adjust to my size.

She wiggles on my dick then uses one of her hands to grab my hair and pull me backwards until I can meet her eyes. "I need you to move. Please move. I'm so full of you, Brett, to the point that I never want to be empty again."

The sincerity and lust shining in her eyes does me in. A sense of pride and possessiveness I have never felt in my life fills me. This woman will warm my bed for as long as I can keep her there.

"You askin' me to fuck you, Morgan?"

Nodding, her sexy, throaty voice says the one thing every man on this planet always wants to hear. "Fuck me until I don't remember what it feels like without you inside of me."

Letting go of her hair, I plant that hand beside her head, and the other hand wraps her thigh around my waist. Then I pull out to my tip and thrust back inside. I might have promised not to fuck her through the mattress, but that didn't mean I wouldn't try to break the fucking bed.

I set a furious rhythm, making sure my pelvis hits her throbbing clit every time I slam home. She starts shuddering under me, the walls of her pussy squeezing me, the tight depths trying to milk my cock. Morgan is screaming hoarse shouts of my name, God, calling me a god, and swearing my dick was a gift from God. Funny, because I am starting to think her pussy is gold dipped and divine.

I am beyond responding to her. Something primitive has taken over, and I am now slamming my cock into her so hard I have to reach back and protect the top of her head from hitting the headboard.

She wanted to never feel empty of me, and I will gladly fuck her until she feels me in her throat. I want to brand her from the inside out. I want to make it so, when she feels me with every little movement she makes, she knows without a doubt that she is mine, and I am hers.

The need to pump harder, faster, deeper overcomes me. I am as wild above her as she is below me.

Her nails rake down my back and break the skin on my ass when she grips there. I love the idea of wearing her marks, feeling those sharp, little erotic pains and knowing this woman is perfect for me.

As I fill her again, she bucks underneath me to meet my thrust. I think there is no way she can get any better.

Then she does.

Morgan Powell, little Miss Prim and Proper, arches her head up and bites the skin just halfway between my ear and the curve of my neck. The barbaric little bite trips my trigger, and I hammer her hard and fast until she lets go of me with her teeth as she becomes a frenzied explosion, her release washing through her.

Her pussy becomes a vise around me, squeezing me until I think I could go blind from the sensations and do nothing except hold on for the ride. It is more pleasure than I have ever felt in my entire life, and I can't wait to experience it again.

Rolling so I won't collapse on top of her, I hold her in my arms, keeping my still pulsing length tucked up inside of her, refusing to pull out yet.

Never do I want to lose her heat.

Never do I want to have her out of my arms.

Never do I want to lose the light that she shines on me and my often dark existence.

Morgan Powell is my very own light at the end of the tunnel, and I didn't have to die to find her.

I know she is close to passing out from exhausted bliss when her sleepy voice says, "Don't forget, Brett. You promised me three times a day." The last word is followed by a small, adorable snore.

A grin spreads across my face until my cheeks start to hurt. Damn, this woman fills all the holes with happiness that I thought had been filled with resignation years ago.

Thank God for cute, stick-up-their-ass women who take their chances on assholes like me.

ICE

Chapter
21

Morgan

One Week Later…

"Well …" Casey probes.

"Well, what?" I answer, playing dumb. I know what she wants; I am simply not convinced I want to tell her here in the club where anyone could overhear us.

"What's it like fuckin' the boss?" she laughs, and I gasp at her crudeness.

"Shhh …" I hiss. "I don't know if anyone is supposed to know about us. And, since you asked so nicely"—I look around to make sure we are alone—"it's amazing. God, why did I wait so long? I know you tried to tell me it would feel good, but I honestly thought you were lying a little. If I had only known it would feel like that, I might not have waited so long after all."

Her fit of giggles has me balling up the paper sitting on the desk in front of me and throwing it at her. It is one thing to admit to yourself that you might have been a naïve idiot about something; it is entirely something else for your best friend to laugh at you about it. With my luck, the next thing out of her mouth will be "I told you so."

Since giving my 'v-card' to Brett, he has been nothing short of amazing. When he has free time, we spend it together. He set me up in his office at After Midnight, and the day I took over the club's books, he was so happy he shut the door and fucked me over the desk. He covered my mouth with his hand because he said he didn't want another man at the club to know just how sweet my screams are. That comment only made me come harder. I don't know why, but I absolutely love how possessive he gets over me.

Since I am here when the girls start arriving for their shifts, Casey tends to come in early to catch up with me. Our friendship has only grown stronger since the day my sister was kidnapped.

When Madyson was missing, she was my sounding board. No matter the time of day or night, if I called, she answered and listened to me yell, cry, or be somber as I went through the emotions of losing my sister. If it were not for Brett and Casey, I would have completely fallen apart.

Brett and I haven't discussed being open about our relationship, and I don't want to overstep my boundaries. I also need to figure out how we will tell Brooke or if Brett intends for us to tell Brooke at all. I know how protective he is over his daughter, and he may be worried about upsetting her. I promised her I would tell her if I ever did have anything with her dad, but now that the situation is here, maybe it is not my place.

Then there is the matter of our age difference. Does it bother him that I am only twenty-four? I know I am young, although many people have told me I have an old soul. I tend to agree with them. Going out clubbing and hooking up with different guys will never be something I want to do. It is obvious I don't do casual relationships. If I did, I would not have held on to my virginity for twenty-four years. A part of me knew I was waiting for the right man. Now, the question is, will the man I think is right for me decide that I am also right for him?

We haven't discussed what he wants in the future. The more I think on it, the more I realize we need to sort it out. The anxiety is building up inside of me, and I am scared of what his answers to my questions may be.

He saved my sister. No matter what the future holds, he will always hold my heart, despite the fact that we started out with a more than a rocky introduction to each other.

As the time passes, there is so much more to Brett 'Ice' Grady than I ever could have imagined. I couldn't pick a better man to give my heart, my body, and everything else I have.

"Look at you, getting all day dreamy over there," Casey jokes.

"He does that to me," I laugh back at her.

"Better be me you're talkin' about when referencing 'he' and doing anything to you," Ice barks out as he enters the office, causing me to blush that he has caught us talking about him.

Casey jumps up out of her seat. "I'm off to get ready for my sets. Catch ya later, girlie!"

Before she can make it out of the office, Ice is pulling me out of my chair and into his hard chest. Tipping my head up, he then kisses me breathless. Sparks fly, fireworks boom—whatever words there are to describe the fire building inside me, it all ignites as he roams my body freely with his hands. He moves to lean against the desk, never breaking contact as he continues his assault on my mouth.

His hand moves to unbutton and unzip my jeans. When he breaks our kiss and moves to nip at my neck, I rock into his hand as he reaches my now damp panties. His fingers push the silken material to the side, and then he inserts one finger in me. With him slowly dragging his finger out of me while also dragging his tongue down my neck, my body is on the edge of seeking release.

His thumb rubs circles on my clit while I put my hands on his shoulders to keep myself steady. I feel myself starting to go weak from the sensations he is building inside of me, never ceasing to be amazed at how he controls my body and the way he is quickly gaining control of my heart.

His tongue swirls on my earlobe before he nips gently. "The door is open. Coal, Skid, or anyone else could walk in right now," he whispers into my ear. His free hand roams up my shirt, his thumb grazing over my erect nipple in my silk bra, giving this unique impression of the feel of his calloused skin on my very soft skin. "I'm gonna set you off right here, right now, and any one of my brothers could come in and see you coming for me." The erotic way he is talking to me, the feel of his finger inside of me, the slow build-up he is creating in me, and the idea that someone could find me here with him only heightens my desire.

I watch the door as if I am willing someone to come, willing someone to watch me fall apart while he takes me higher and higher. I am so turned on I would beg him to keep going no matter who came in.

"So wet for me, all for me. If they come in, they will watch you fall apart for me. This is all mine," he states as he adds pressure with his thumb and pushes two fingers to pump in and out of me.

I grip his shoulders as his hand in my shirt pulls my left breast out of my bra. It isn't comfortable, but it is far from uncomfortable as I get lost in the response that only he can pull from me.

Brett pulls back his head, keeping one hand working me and moving my shirt up to expose me with the other. When his hot mouth comes down and sucks on my nipple, I feel myself clenching around his fingers as I hold his head against me. He stills the fingers inside me as I ride out my orgasm.

Once the aftershocks subside, he pulls his fingers free of me, and I reluctantly release my grip on him and steady myself on my feet. I tuck my boob back into my bra, and he flashes an unrepentant smile at me as he pulls my shirt down for me.

A knock at the doorway freezes every muscle in my body. Although I am still coming down from my orgasm, I am cognizant enough to realize my pants are still undone. Hammer sits in his wheelchair with a knowing smirk as I feel a blush creep over me. Even though I am hidden by Brett's body, I can't help but feel like Hammer knows what we were just doing.

"Ice, we got a meeting in thirty."

Ice watches me, not responding to Hammer, and brings the fingers he just took out of me to his mouth to lick them. With his back to Hammer, knowing he is tasting me on his skin while his friend watches, I get excited all over again.

What has this man done to me? Not in a million years would I have ever imagined ending up with someone who wants to be watched while engaging in intimate acts. There is something about Brett that throws all of my inhibitions out the window to become road kill on the highway called life. He brings out a wildness in me I never knew was there.

And I love it.

"I'll be ready in five," he says, licking his lips without taking his eyes off me.

"Sure thing," Hammer says, smiling at me. "I'll expect you in fifteen, then." He laughs for the first time since getting out of rehabilitation from his accident. "And about that conversation I once said we were gonna have about Miss Prim and Proper shakin' you up…I don't think we need to talk anymore." He laughs more and Ice smiles over his shoulder at his friend.

There is a long road to recovery ahead for him and my sister. Together, however, with the support of the family that is the Regulators MC, I think they will both come out on the other side okay.

I would have never pictured myself doing accounting for two strip clubs or sleeping with the president of a motorcycle club, but then again, the best things are sometimes the least expected. Things aren't always what they seem, and everything about this club is about family, loyalty, and protecting what is theirs.

My bad to the bone man is quite possibly one of the greatest things that could have ever happened to my life.

ICE

Chapter

22

Ice

"So, let me get this straight, Dad. You and Morgan, you're a couple?" Brooke asks.

Once again, I am in uncharted waters with my teenage daughter. I am trying to have a conversation with her about my new relationship. The way she is watching me right now almost feels like she is the proverbial shark, circling me, waiting for the moment I screw up so she can strike. There is no telling what is going on through this child's head. I am almost positive I would not want to know anyways.

"That's what I said."

"Okay, so how is it that we had the 'talk' a few years back,"—she pauses for dramatic effect, only making me relive the awkward sex chat with her all over again—"and in that 'talk' you told me don't give it up easily. Just because a boy takes me out, he isn't worthy, you know, of all that shit."

"Language," I chastise.

"Yup. Again, so I can't 'give it up,' as you say, without actually dating the dude for a while, like a long while … again, as you say, 'make them work for it, earn it,' you know, don't just give the gift away."

"Land your plane, Brooke. What is your point?" I snap. Trying to talk to a teenager sometimes is enough to drive any person bat-shit crazy.

"I like Morgan—really, really like her—and I want her to be around. I actually think she is perfect for you, for us even. She fills this space with stuff that I didn't even know we were missing until she was here. Dad, she like, makes the best cookies. She helps me with *math*! She doesn't get frustrated with me." Her eyes glare dramatically at me, trying to get her point across. "She is everything I would truly want for you and for us as a family."

"Great," I say, feeling relieved that she is happy about this.

"Not great. Dad, what are you doing for Morgan? Do you know she says you are the example to what I should hold my boyfriends to? She goes on and on about how you take care of me, protect me, provide for me, and you are always here to listen or just be with me. All of which is true. Whatever man I do finally settle down with—"

"When you're older. Much. Fuckin'. Older," I interrupt to remind her she is too young to even think of being serious with a boy.

"Dad, stop redirecting and listen to me. What are you doing for Morgan?"

"What do you mean?" I know damn well what I do for Morgan and her body.

"You haven't taken her on ONE fuckin' date!" Brooke fusses and pushes at my shoulder.

My mind swirls so fast I don't even bother giving her a lecture on her language. Shit, my kid is right. I have fucked this up already.

Without hesitation, I grab my phone. I know it is early on a Saturday morning, and she was up late because of my visit, but this is important.

"Ice," she greets groggily into the phone.

"Be ready at six tonight."

"Umm ... I haven't exactly had coffee yet, honey, so can you tell me exactly what I need to be ready for?"

"Our first date."

"Umm ... okay." She pauses. "Is this for real?"

"Yeah, sweetheart, I'm bein' real. I was talkin' to Brooke about us—"

"Brooke knows," she gasps. "Is she mad at me? I should've talked to her first."

"She is fine with you. She likes you, Morgan. This is about us. I've treated you wrong, and now I need to make that right, both for you and for her. Apparently, she took your 'I'm the example' talk to heart, and I'm not being a very good standard for her to hold the pimple faced pricks surrounding her up to. Tonight, I rectify that. We're goin' out, sweetheart."

She laughs into the phone as Brooke grabs it out of my hand.

"Forget him. Come over with Madyson. I'll send Dad away. We'll have girl time together, getting you ready for your hot date, and Madyson can stay here with me while y'all are out. This way, you both know she's safe, she will feel safe, and you two can go out with no worries."

While my teen daughter squeals into the phone, before taking off down the hall, still talking to my woman about what outfits to bring over and how she's going to do her hair, I can't help snorting. It appears I didn't have to worry about Brooke and Morgan getting along.

As I think on it, Brooke's words stand out to me.

She fills this space with stuff that I didn't even know we were missing until she was here.

She is right. I smile more. I relax more. Overall, since Morgan Ann Powell came into my life, I find myself happier. For the first time since Erin died, I feel like there is more to my life than being a dad, a soldier, or a Regulator.

The innocent woman that exudes kindness, in a cute way that is uniquely hers, has come into my life and turned it all upside down. I don't want to be without her. On first appearances, I never would have thought she could handle my lifestyle. Things aren't always what they seem, though, are they?

Her sister was missing and she faced it head on, refusing to give up even when she didn't have a clue what she was doing. She challenged me at every turn, never bowing down or taking my shit, even when I was a complete asshole, which was often. She was made for me in a way I don't know if Erin ever was, because I was too young to notice.

Morgan isn't afraid of taking on Brooke and her teenage tantrums. She has handled her with love, patience, and understanding. Rather than turn her back on her sister, she embraced her and took on her problems as her own. Even more so, the woman is already trying to figure out how to rescue her other sister from the clutches of her crazy-ass parents. The woman was born to be a maternal figure. She just has not realized it yet.

Morgan is exactly what I need without even recognizing it, just like Brooke said. My chest tightens as I let that sink in. Maybe the powers that be decided I needed a second chance at life to have someone, besides my daughter, who makes it worth living.

Morgan

What the hell have I gotten myself into?

Butterflies tango in my belly as my nerves build up. On one hand, I can say this is happening fast. On the other hand, I have known Ice for months now, and he has been a rock solid source of strength for me. It feels like a whirlwind romance in the sense of our relationship, but the reality is, he was my friend first. It is a friendship that started off a little rocky yet has grown into something beautiful.

I have come to realize, during our short time together, that he is it for me.

His actions have proven he will always be there to catch me when I fall. I know it with every fiber of my being. He doesn't play games. I never wonder or worry if I am enough for him when he is surrounded by gorgeous women at the club. He makes sure to show me, in a variety of creative ways, precisely how much he wants me and only me.

With Ice, what I see is what I get, no apologies. He brings out the sassy side of me. I want to challenge him because he has shown me I am strong-willed enough to do it. I don't want to simply take whatever shit he dishes out. And, when I do throw my attitude around to let him know he has crossed a line, he gets this look on his face that lets me know he is proud to call me his. He balances me in a way I never imagined a lover would. Now that I have that from him, I can't imagine living a life without it.

As I sit at his daughter's vanity, while she curls my hair into soft tendrils around my face, I anxiously wonder what tonight will bring. A date with Ice? I can't imagine. Will we end up at a biker bar? Ride his bike all night long? Go to After Midnight and watch his girls strip?

As much as I love spending time with him, I can't imagine Brett 'Ice' Grady going on a date. That has to be against some sort of rule in the 'Bad-ass Biker Bible,' right?

"Are you excited?" Brooke asks me.

I wish I could nod my head, instead of answering, so she wouldn't hear the nervousness in my voice, but I cannot move since she is still curling my hair.

"Yeah. What do you think your dad is planning, anyways?"

Brooke giggles, and the sound has me looking up in her mirror to see her mischievous eyes glowing. It reminds me of the look Ice gives me when he is feeling playful.

"I'm not telling," she answers me smugly.

"Brat."

She rolls her eyes. "Like I haven't heard that one before. Just remember, when you think you have Dad figured out, he's always going to do something to prove that you don't."

Boy, isn't that the statement of the century.

"Where's Madyson?" I ask when I see she is almost finished with my hair.

"Out in the living room, watching TV with Dad."

"Are you sure you two will be okay here tonight?" I can't help worrying about my little sister. Although she has come a long way, shadows still plague her eyes, and the nightmares seem to never end.

"*Pfft*. Do you really think Dad would leave us here alone? One of the boys is probably already here, waiting to start babysitting duty." She rolls her eyes again. "Because grown men just love to sit around and hear teenage girls talk clothes and make-up."

I giggle as I wonder which poor soul Ice is torturing tonight. I know it's not Hammer, because he is still wheelchair bound and never goes anywhere except to his house and the club for business.

Putting the curling iron down on her vanity, Brooke fluffs my hair one last time. "You ready?"

I nod while studying myself in the mirror. My make-up isn't much darker than what I wear to work, the eye shadow a shimmery golden brown with a thick line of dark brown eyeliner to compliment my green eyes. My lips are painted a satin rose mauve color, and I can't help wondering what it will look like on Ice's lips after I give him a kiss sometime later tonight.

I look down to see the white knitted top with a subtle icy glimmer to it. From the top up, I look like the prim and proper Morgan that Ice likes to joke about dirtying up all the time. From the bottom down is a whole different story. I am wearing an over-the-knee black leather pencil skirt paired with wicked crystal-silver and black leather, stiletto-heeled, peep-toe ankle boots.

Morgan and Madyson went shopping with me today, and the minute Madyson spotted the boots, she said I needed them for tonight. She told me, with the rest of the outfit, I would look like a frosty, yet tempting, little She Devil to compliment the man who is as icy as his name.

Looking at my outfit, I have to admit she was right. Now, what will the man I call mine think? It is time to find out.

Walking out of Brooke's room and down the hall to the living room, the sound of my heels click against the hardwood floor, undoubtedly warning whoever is out there of my impending arrival. When I emerge from the hallway, it is to find Madyson sitting on the couch with Ice while Coal sits in the adjacent chair.

Madyson gives me a huge grin that warms my heart. I haven't seen her smile in such a way since before she was rescued. I would do anything to see that smile again every day.

Coal smirks at my appearance. "Only you could look like a fairy princess wearing leather, woman."

"Take your eyes off my woman, jackass," Ice orders as he gets up from the couch and heads towards me in what is definitely a predatory stalk instead of a normal stride. The heavy muscles throughout his body flex under his tight black T-shirt. His low slung jeans cling to his thick thighs, cupping the erection I can plainly see. With the way he is looking at me, I wonder if we will make it out the door at all.

When he grabs me by my hips, he slowly runs his hands over the leather that clings to me until he is cupping my ass, I can't help the shiver of arousal that runs through me. The man before me is potent, virile. He makes me want to go to the bedroom and stay in there for days … or weeks. Months even.

Leaning forward, he whispers into my ear, "All of this for me, baby? A pretty present for me to unwrap later?"

My mouth goes dry at the insinuation. I can barely squeak out, "Yes, Brett."

"Good," he rumbles. "I might not unwrap everything, though. I might leave you in that sexy leather. I'll strip that cute little top off until I can see what I bet is one of your innocent lookin' white lace bras, and then

I'm gonna bend you over my bed and fuck you until you're screaming my name."

My breath catches in my chest as I envision his words, my panties dampening with desire. I can't stop myself from asking him, "Are you sure we have to go on a date?"

He pulls back and chuckles at my flushed cheeks. "Damn right we do, sweetheart. I'm gonna take my woman out, act like a gentleman, and then bring her home and give her the caveman."

"Ewww, Dad. No sexin' where others can see you!" his daughter complains from behind us.

His mouth tips in a smirk, and he leans forwards to murmur so only I can hear him. "But my woman likes it when others might see us."

I groan in need, making him laugh. Then he grabs my hand and drags me towards the front door, waving at Coal and ordering the girls to be good while we are gone. Pulling me to his truck, he avoids the passenger side and takes me straight to the driver's side instead.

Opening the door, he lifts me up to the bench seat. "Scoot over a little, baby, and let me get in, but don't go too far. I wanna feel you pressed up against me as I drive."

God, this man knows how to make my heart do somersaults in my chest.

I slip over, giving him enough room to get in, and then we cruise down the street on four wheels instead of the two he usually rides on, which feels weird; however, tonight is all about going with the flow, to see what my man considers a date. If we pull up to his strip club, though, I might have to cook him something he chokes on.

We don't end up at the club, though. Nor do we end up at a bar or anything else I have dreamed up that a rugged man like Ice might visit. No, we park at a four star restaurant, and I feel my jaw drop.

Looking over to Ice, I ask, flabbergasted, "Are you sure we're in the right place?"

"Yep."

Pulling me out of the truck, he walks us into the elegant building and gives the hostess his name. The young girl gives him a bright smile in return, grabs two menus, and then leads us back to a secluded corner with candles lit and roses in a vase on the table. Ice pulls out my chair for me then takes the chair across from me as the hostess babbles about the night's specials.

Once she leaves, my mind stops swirling enough to ask Ice another question. "Why would you bring me here?"

He cocks an eyebrow at my question, and I realize how ungrateful I sound. "That's not how I meant it, I swear. I'm so sorry. I just—" I can't stop stammering. "I just didn't expect you to bring me to some place like this!" I whisper-yell at him.

Amused by my reaction, that cocky smile spreads across his face. "You want to know why I brought you here, Morgan?"

I shake my head. I wouldn't have asked if I knew why we were here.

Leaning forward to rest his elbows on the table, he answers me softly, "I'm gonna wine you and dine you like you deserve, sweetheart."

My heart melts. Every day, he finds a way to surprise me with his actions or words, opening himself up to me little by little. Can this man get any better?

Then that familiar Grady mischievous look sparkles in his eyes, and he adds, "But, when we're done here, I'm gonna take you somewhere and fuck you in the truck like I deserve."

Yes, apparently my man can get better.

He orders dinner and wine for us when the waiter shows up. We eat our delicious food, talk about Madyson and Brooke, and simply spend time enjoying each other's company. When we are done, he pays, we leave, and by the time we reach the truck, my anticipation for what comes next is already boiling inside of me.

After we climb up into the truck and Ice starts to drive back through town, I put my hand on his thigh and start to rub up and down his leg.

"Where are we going?"

"That's for me to know, and you to worry about until we get there."

"What does that mean, Ice?"

"That means we're going to play naughty, baby, and we start right now. I want you to slide that tight skirt of yours down until it's around your ankles."

I gasp. "But what if someone sees us?"

The lights along the street light up his face enough that I can see his smile. "That's the point, Morgan—someone might see us. Now do what I say."

My heart is thumping so hard in my chest I wonder if he can hear it. Unzipping the side of my skirt, I grab both sides and inch the tight leather down my thighs, little by little, until I am finally able to slide it down my legs to the floorboard.

Ice groans low in his throat beside me. "Sweet little white lace panties to cover my sweet little pussy. Pull the crotch of your panties aside and play with yourself. I want you nice and wet before I stop this truck."

I do what he tells me, both terrified that someone might see me petting myself and exhilarated by the thought. It does not take long until I am on the edge of an orgasm, my head resting on the back of the seat, moaning from the pleasure.

"Don't you dare come yet, Morgan. I want my cock inside you when you come so I can feel it squeezing my dick."

I whine, almost in pain from the intense pleasure and his command to wait for him. "Hurry, Brett. Please, please hurry. I need to come so badly. How much longer?"

"We're here."

I peel my eyelids open to see where 'here' is. It is almost unbelievable what meets my eyes.

"A drive-in movie theater?" I ask, baffled.

Two of Brett's fingers suddenly fill me, and my head whips back at the sensation of being filled. "I gave you dinner, now you're gonna give me a show. Damn, you're clenching my fingers already. Get your ass over here."

He pulls his fingers out as I look at his lap to see the long, thick, engorged flesh is already covered in a condom. I can't believe I am about to do this. Having sex in the club's office with the door open is one thing; having sex in a truck surrounded by other vehicles filled with people is entirely different. The only thing that comforts me is that all of his windows, except the windshield, are darkly tinted.

"Stop procrastinating, Morgan, and get on my dick."

I move over him, situating my knees on either side of his lap, maneuvering myself over him. He grabs my hips, steadying me, while I grab him in my hand and position him at my entrance. Once I have him where I want him, I slowly slide down his length. Now it is his head that rests on the top of the seat.

"Damn you feel so good around me, baby. Hot, tight, wet little pussy that squeezes and sucks me better than any fuckin' dream I've ever had."

His words spurn me to move faster, ride him harder. It is not easy in the cramped space of the truck cab, but now that he fills me in the most delicious way, I can't stop.

I feel it building in me again, that glorious peak only Brett can make me feel.

"God, Brett. So good. So, so good."

"Fuck yeah," he responds. "Ride me good, sweetheart."

My body bucks uncontrollably as that erotic rush starts to fill me. I try to muffle my scream by biting my bottom lip, but a loud moan escapes me anyways. My legs start to go weak as I explode around him, and Brett takes over for me.

Gripping my hips in a strong hold, he picks me up and slams me down on his cock once, twice, three times before he growls his release.

My entire body melts. I can't move, and I don't want to. We stay like that for who knows how long, holding each other, reveling in the way we make each other feel. Eventually, though, he lifts me off him, places me gently on the seat next to him, and takes care of the condom. Then he buckles my seatbelt and pulls me tightly into his side, cuddling me. Neither one of us says a word as he starts up his truck to leave the theater grounds.

Once we finally make it home, I do my best not to flush when Coal, Madyson, and Brooke's eyes turn from the TV to us. Coal flat out grins at my disheveled appearance, but the girls don't seem to notice.

"So what did you two do?" Madyson asks.

I can't make myself open my mouth to answer the question. Never in a million years will I tell my little sister what we did.

Ice squeezes me to his side and chuckles. "Dinner and a movie."

Oh, my God, I'll never be able to face that drive-in theater again.

Epilogue

Morgan

A little over a year later…

"Madyson, if you want to get ready at Brooke's, babe, we gotta go," I yell down the hall to my sister.

"Okay, I'm almost ready!"

In the kitchen, I watch as she comes out of her room with her garment bag holding her dress, cap, and gown as well as her makeup bag. Her hair is up in curlers, her face glowing with a new maturity.

The last year hasn't been easy, but she has made it through. After her attendance was beyond recovery, she dropped out of high school. Although I offered to let her finish online in a homeschool program, she refused.

I feel the prick of tears, yet manage to hold them back. Madyson does not like it when someone looks at her in pity, and she really does not like it when I cry. Her new attitude is that of a survivor. The past is the past, and all she wants to do is look forward to her future.

"You know I'm proud of you, right, Mady?"

"Yes, Morgan, you tell me all the damn time," she huffs in mock exasperation.

"Not many girls could do what you did. After everything, you went back to school, knowing people were talking. You held your head high and focused on your studies. A lot of women would've tucked their tail between their legs and stayed home, never venturing out of their house again. Mady, I can't say I could do what you've done."

I wipe the tears that finally leak from my eyes as I stare at my sister in awe of her courage and strength to endure and overcome. She is the strongest person I have ever met, though still so young. I thank God every day that He gave me the chance to have her in my life after her ordeal.

We have grown very close in the past year, learning how family is supposed to love instead of acting how our parents raised us.

She rushes over to me, dropping the bag, and wraps her arms tightly around my body. We both cry together for a few moments until she pulls away to look up at me.

"I wouldn't have survived without you, Morgan. My strength comes from you. No one else would've stuck by my side, yet you never left me. Today is as much about you as it is me. When I walk across that stage, I take every step knowing you are stepping with me. Every day I wake up, I wake up knowing you wake up for me. You took care of me when our parents wouldn't, loved me when they wouldn't. You lost your job because you wouldn't give up on finding me. You did all this for me; so today, I get that diploma for us both. Without you, I would've died. There were days, while I was going through withdrawals that I *wanted* to die. The only thing that kept me going was the squeeze of your hand around my own to remind me that I wasn't alone."

Sniffling, I try to compose myself. "Remember when we were little? When Mallory would get on our nerves, we would say 'It's you and me against the world' and run away from her?" She nods her head against me, squeezing me tightly. "It's always you and me against the world, Mady. Only now, we will say it's us against the world and take Mallory with us." I smile sweetly at her, knowing that Mallory will soon be with us.

Madyson going back to school gave them daily opportunities to talk. I couldn't take on Mallory with Madyson still recovering; however, now that she is rock solid, thanks to the help of an amazing therapist Coal found, we are planning to have Mallory move in over the summer. Mom and Dad are losing their house to foreclosure, anyway. Mal says Mom is threatening divorce.

It won't be easy taking on another teenager, but it will be worth it to have my other sister with us.

Madyson reaches up and wipes my tears away as she smiles back at me. "Let's go," she whispers happily.

We pack my car with everything she needs before driving over to Ice's house. By the time we get there, I see Ice's eye twitching as he opens the front door. I can hear Brooke in the background, yelling about something.

Reaching out with both hands, he grabs each of us around our wrists then pulls us into the house. After slamming the door, he looks at Madyson and barks, "Love my baby girl, but honest to God, if you don't go back there and calm her shit down, I'm going to duct tape her mouth shut."

Madyson bites her bottom lip in an effort not to giggle and nods her head at him before scurrying to the back of the house.

When she disappears out of sight, Ice looks back to me, takes one look at my smiling face, and growls. "This shit ain't funny. And, if I catch you laughing at me, I'm gonna make you regret it."

Propping my hands on my hips, I egg him on. "Yeah? How you gonna do that, big boy?"

"By cutting you down from gettin' my dick three times a day to once a week. Then we'll see who's laughin'." The gleam in his eyes tells me he is dead serious about that threat.

I walk past him without saying a word, back to his daughter's room where I can keep myself out of trouble. When a woman gets it as good as I do, you definitely do not want to get cut off.

After hours of watching Brooke and Mady do hair, makeup, get dressed, and giggle like crazy, we are finally ready to head out. We get there to find the high school is packed with parents and students excited for the journey ahead. The Regulators are all in attendance, Harleys lined up in the parking lot.

Getting out of Ice's new SUV, I smile at the two girls as I watch my man proudly wrap his daughter in a hug.

"Ice!" I hear called out from our left.

Both Ice and his daughter look over, and then Brooke screams, "Uncle Shooter," and takes off running.

A tall, built man with short, spiked blonde hair hugs her as a gorgeous brunette stands behind him with a young boy holding her hand. Grabbing my hand, Ice tugs me along to meet the man his daughter is talking to.

After they do that man half-hug, back slap thing, the blonde man smiles at me.

"Shooter, this is Morgan," Ice introduces us.

"Damn, never thought I'd see the day someone melted that permafrost around your heart. Congrats, asshole," Shooter jokes while extending his hand to me.

I give his hand a quick, friendly shake before stepping back next to Ice. My man made it clear a long time ago he did not like other men touching me. That includes innocent gestures, even from his friends, like the one who is giving me a knowing smile now at my actions.

"Fuck you!" Ice replies in jest while wrapping his arm around my shoulders.

Shooter also steps back and wraps his arm around the woman he brought with him. "Brooke, Ice, this is my ol' lady, Tessie, and our boy Axel."

"Nice to meet you in person after talking on the phone so much." Brooke bounces excitedly. "I can't believe you're actually here, Uncle Shooter."

"Wouldn't miss it for the world, baby girl."

"She's got the ring, so when are you givin' her the name?" Ice asks Shooter, nodding at Tessie's left hand.

"As soon as she gives me a day and time to show up," he proudly answers. Nodding my way, he says, "You better move that one in before someone else swoops in and snatches that prize right out of your hands." Shooter gives me a playful wink.

"Just needed to get these two graduated. After today, that's a definite, brother."

Did he just say what I think he said?

My jaw drops open in surprise for a second while I turn my head to face him and poke him in the chest with my finger. "Excuse me. I'm not moving in with you."

"Why the fuck not?" Ice asks, and I can hear Madyson and Brooke start to laugh behind us.

"You haven't even managed to tell me you love me, and we've been together for over a year; why in the hell would I move in with you?"

His entire demeanor changes from one of joking to complete seriousness. He turns to me, cupping my face in both of his hands, forcing me to meet his stare. "I'm a man of actions because they speak louder than words. Sweetheart, you want the words, you need the words, you got them. I told you, once I see something I want, I don't let it go. Morgan, I love you. I love you yesterday, I love you today, I love you tomorrow, and I will love you for the rest of my days."

The world around us seems to disappear. All I can see is the way his eyes glow with the depths of his emotions. Tears pool in my own eyes at hearing him say

{}

exactly what I have needed, what I have longed to hear for months now.

Forgetting that we are surrounded by hundreds of people, including our family and friends, I fist his shirt in both of my hands and rise up on my tiptoes so we are standing nose to nose. "Kiss me."

"No. Say yes first," he argues back.

"Yes to what?" I challenge.

"Moving in."

"I like it better when you tell me what I'm doing," I reply, sassily, with a wink.

He smirks at my innuendo at his bossiness in and out of the bedroom.

Not wanting to ruin our moment, yet knowing it needs to be said, I give him the truth. I have to look out for my family, no matter how much I love the man in front of me. "It's not just me, though."

As always, what he says next surprises me. "Sweetheart, my house is big enough for you, your sisters, my daughter, and the babies you're gonna give me. Why the hell do you think I bought the SUV? I needed somethin' big enough to tote all my girls around in."

"I'm givin' you babies, huh?" I zero in on the most surprising statement of all and smile lovingly at him.

"Yeah, after you tell me you love me, you kiss me, we get two diplomas for our girls, we spend some time with my friends, and you move in. Then, sweetheart, we are workin' on baby makin'."

"How fast am I moving in?"

"Tomorrow," he answers adamantly. "Me and the boys will be at your place bright and early with our vans to pack you up and get you settled at my place."

"What about my lease on the condo?"

"It's about to run out, and you're sure as shit not renewing. You're meant to be in my bed every night, not halfway across town every other night. You got any other questions?"

"Since you caught me up on the plan now, I think I can oblige," I answer with a wide, playful grin. Then, biting my bottom lip shyly, I give him the words I have waited patiently to say to him. "I love you, Brett."

"About damn time," he growls.

Before I can say another word, his lips crash down on mine, fulfilling the next step in his plans. With the man I love wrapped around me, literally surrounding me with his warmth and love, I am more than ready to go through each and every one of his steps with him for the rest of our days.

~*The End*~

Things aren't always what they seem.

There is nothing regular about the Regulators MC. Sometimes we don't realize we were missing something in our lives until we have it. Join us next as Hammer copes with overcoming his injuries. He is not prepared to not only rebuild his body, but his life as well.

Lucas Young, Riley and Kara Sullivan, and the rest of the Ex Ops team can be found in Secret Maneuvers and Stripping Her Defenses by Jessie Lane.

Shooter can be found in The Hellions Ride series by Chelsea Camaron.

About the Authors

Chelsea Camaron

Chelsea Camaron was born and raised in Coastal North Carolina. She currently resides in Louisiana with her husband and two children but her heart is always Carolina day dreaming.

Chelsea always wanted to be a writer, but like most of us, let fear of the unknown grab a hold of her dream; she realized that if she was going to tell her daughter to go for her dreams, that it was time to follow her own advice.

Chelsea grew up turning wrenches alongside her father, and from that grew her love for old muscle cars and Harley Davidson motorcycles. This just so happened to inspired her 'Love and Repair' and 'The Hellions Ride' series.

When she is not spending her days writing you can find her playing with her kids, attending car shows, going on motorcycle rides on the back of her husband's Harley, snuggling down with her new favorite book or watching any movie that Vin Diesel might happen to be in.

For more information on Chelsea Camaron:
www.authorchelseacamaron.com

Or you can send Chelsea Camaron an email at:
chelseacamaron@gmail.com

Jessie Lane

Jessie Lane is the best-selling author of The Star Series, Big Bad Bite Series and the Ex Ops Series. She writes paranormal and contemporary romance, as well as Upper YA Paranormal Romance/Fantasy.

She lives in Kentucky with her two little Rock Chicks in the making and her over protective alpha husband. She has a passionate love for reading and writing naughty romance, cliff hanging suspense, and out-of-this-world characters that demand your attention, or threaten to slap you around until you do pay attention to them.

For more information on Jessie Lane:
http://jessielanebooks.com

Or you can send Jessie Lane an email at:
jessie_lane@jessielanebooks1.com

ICE

You May Also Like

Also available from Chelsea Camaron & Jessie Lane!